UNDERCOVER MARSHAL

The town of Dry Acres is under the oppression of a crooked alliance between outlaw Mark Grayson and his protector, Mayor and Sheriff Henry Binalt. When the local newspaper editor, Gil Radford, is murdered before he can expose the corruption, his niece, Ann Dalman, resolves to carry on his fight. She calls in Radford's friend, Blake Carson, to help. To protect his secret interests, Binalt then hires a notorious gunman to eliminate Carson. But there is an unexpected result . . .

RUSSELL JAMES

UNDERCOVER MARSHAL

Complete and Unabridged

LINFORD
Leicester

First published in Great Britain in 2002 by
Robert Hale Limited, London
Based on a short story by John Russell Fearn

First Linford Edition
published 2004
by arrangement with
Robert Hale Limited, London

The moral right of the author has been asserted
Any resemblance between any character appearing in this novel and any person living or dead is entirely coincidental and unintentional.

British Library CIP Data

James, Russell
    Undercover marshal.—Large print ed.—
Linford western library
1. Large type books
2. Western stories
I. Title
823.9'14 [F]

ISBN 1–84395–167–3

Published by
F. A. Thorpe (Publishing)
Anstey, Leicestershire

Set by Words & Graphics Ltd.
Anstey, Leicestershire
Printed and bound in Great Britain by
T. J. International Ltd., Padstow, Cornwall

This book is printed on acid-free paper

1

'If a man can't print the truth, Ann, he ain't fit to smell the ink. If a man can't expose to this tyrant-ridden town the real facts about the feller runnin' it, you an' me just shouldn't be here! That's the top'n bottom of it.'

Gil Radford had said this many times, but never with quite such vehemence. He spoke now like a man who can no longer contain a secret.

Ann Dalman looked across at him from the type-rack. Her uncle was standing in the offices of the *Dry Acres Gazette* by the partly open window, staring on to the dusty street shimmering in the blaze of afternoon sun.

The small town of Dry Acres, within seeing distance of mountains on every side, lay cupped in a hollow and as such was the target for merciless sunshine and hot, arid winds.

'I'm goin' to print it!' Gil Radford thumped a decisive hand on the ledge of the window. 'It may finish me — but if we don't expose Mark Grayson and all his works this town'll just go on sizzlin' and sweatin' and doin' as he tells it.'

He moved agitatedly from the window and Ann kept her eyes upon him as he came towards her. She knew he meant it this time.

There was resolution in his tired blue eyes, firmness in the creases of his weather-beaten face. And, as Ann knew, when her uncle made up his mind he acted with all the hard-hitting determination which had made him take to the trails very early in life. He was grey-haired and less agile now, but the old fires still burned.

'Do you have to take such a chance, uncle?' Ann asked, catching at his arm before he reached the desk. 'Just think for a moment — Nothing happens to you as long as you print the news Grayson approves of. You get just

2

enough out of the paper to get by. Why throw it all away just to be . . . honest?'

Her uncle studied her from under grizzled brows. He saw a face still young and passing pretty, with very grey eyes and light-blonde hair. Ann was a combination of his brother-in-law and his sister, Ann's mother. She had been killed in a cattle stampede when Ann had been only a year old. Ever since, her uncle had been her close friend and confidant.

'Like the rest of these half-fried folk in Dry Acres, you're scared o' Grayson, Ann,' he told her. 'Not as I blame you — after what he did to your dad's ranch. He's a tin-horn dictator and can get away with most things, 'specially since we got that useless sheriff we have nowadays. But he's gotten away with it long enough and we're runnin' a news-sheet which is supposed to tell the truth. 'Sides, I think I know who Mark Grayson really is . . . '

Radford sat down at the desk and clenched his fists on it.

'I'm goin' to give this cockeyed town the biggest jolt it's ever had, Ann! I'm goin' to tell 'em who Grayson really is; how he diverted the watercourse from your father's Roaring G spread; how he's trod on men and women's faces to get where he is now; how he's shot the daylights out of everybody who's tried to block him . . . '

'We've been hard hit, I know,' Ann interrupted. 'Our cattle's poor and the pasture dry because of that diverted watercourse, and we know Grayson's climbed up over other people. But we haven't the *proof* of it! If we had then it would amount to something. As it is it's just words — and dangerous words, because Mark Grayson isn't the sort to let you get away with them!'

'Listen, Ann . . . ' her uncle caught her hand, 'I'm goin' to write and print this editorial exposé because I think it's right and proper. I'd sooner die shoutin' the truth than concealin' it. I'm no longer young enough to fight it out with a sixgun as I'd have done once; my power now is in the pen. But if somethin' should happen to me, as likely may, your job will be to carry on and do all you can to show up Grayson for what he is.'

'Unless I get wiped out, too!' Ann's voice was quiet, but her uncle shook his head.

'Not *you*, Ann. Mark Grayson won't do that; I happen to know he's got a soft spot in his hard heart for you. But listen, if I should suffer for what I'm going to do — after the paper is published — you'll need outside help. I've fixed it all up. Here's what you must do . . . '

★   ★   ★

It was late afternoon when Ann left the print shop. The editorial had been written and set up in type. Within the hour Ann would return with tea for her uncle and herself and then help him to get the issue out ready for the following morning.

As she made her way through the torrid little town with its dust and false fronts she could not help but reflect upon the oppression that nailed it down. The cause of it all was Mark Grayson, owner of the Black Slipper saloon at the far end of the street.

A close friend of Henry Binalt, the town's sheriff and mayor, Grayson was a dealer in real-estate, lawyer, gambler — he had a finger in everything and a hired gun for awkward questions.

Those who did not work with him were scared of him, had been ever since that flaming hot day three years ago when his shadow had first fallen across Dry Acres.

The ramshackle town had never aimed at being anything more than a cattle exchange anyway, but since the coming of Grayson it had become other things besides. There was mysterious business that only he knew about: the selling of illegal hides, for one thing; the exchange of cattle foreign to the Dry Acres corrals for another. And until now nobody had raised any eyebrows. Until now!

Ann Dalman thought of her uncle and she tightened her lips ... She continued up the main street, watched by the idling cowpunchers from the boardwalks of the crazy little buildings, and so presently she left the centre of the town and hurried over the dusty scrub to where her father's Roaring G ranch stood.

There were a few weary cattle in the rope corral, cattle that could have become sleek and healthy but for the diversion of the watercourse.

Grayson had done this when Ann's father, Bruce Dalman, had said too much soon after Grayson's arrival in town. Dalman's appeals to the law had got nowhere.

Henry Binalt, who had followed Grayson into the town not long after his arrival, was Grayson's close friend. He seemed reluctant to hear a word against him. Now the watercourse was dammed by a high bank of concrete and scrub and turned its precious gleaming thread towards Grayson's own prosperous Flying F spread further down the valley.

With bitter thoughts Ann ascended the steps to the porch of the ranch, pulled open the screen door and went inside. In perhaps fifteen minutes she came out again, carrying in a basket the necessities for her own and her uncle's tea.

Old Ginger Kenyon, the one cowhand who had remained faithful through the decline of fortune, was just slipping the reins of his horse over the corral fence.

'Afternoon, ma'am!' He touched the brim of his faded sombrero as the girl came towards him. 'I reckon you'll be wantin' me to take on as usual?'

'As usual, Ginger,' Ann agreed, sighing. 'Ask my father to get Steve and Ralph to help you. Uncle and I have a paper to put to bed in town.'

Ginger hesitated as though he could not quite understand her mood. Doubt was in his sun-gnarled face and narrowed eyes. It was as if he could sense her disquiet. But as she said no more he shrugged and turned away.

At length Ann was back in the print shop just as her uncle was lifting the editorial page-proof from the wet type.

'That's it, m'girl!' he declared, with an admiring wag of his head. 'The whole thing!'

'Can I read it?' she asked eagerly.

'Sure you can! Here you . . .'

The doorbell clanged abruptly. Ann turned in surprise — and in some annoyance, for so far she had not seen the exposé her uncle had been engaged upon. Now this interruption . . . Her uncle lowered the sheet and slanted a blue eye.

Against the sunlight streaming through the doorway stood a hard-faced cow-puncher, his hand resting on his holster.

'Well, Curly, what do *you* want?' Gil Radford asked the question casually as he laid the proof-sheet on one side.

'You!' Curly Mitchell answered. He came forward slowly, hat tilted over his small eyes, his mouth a compressed scar. He was one of Grayson's best gunmen, and proud of it.

'And what should you be wantin' with me?' Radford asked, turning calmly to face him.

'Yuh got it all figured to plaster the town with that editorial, ain't you?' Curly asked, coming forward and snatching up the proof-sheet from where it lay on a table. 'Yuh should be more careful, Radford. A voice gets around easy through that open window.' He smiled slyly. 'I heard yuh talkin' with Miss Ann here, see. I told the boss what yuh said, an' it seems he don't kinda like notions like yourn.'

Ann darted a fearful glance towards her uncle's grim face, then back to Curly again. His knotted fingers had tightened on the butt of his sixgun.

'I guess I forgot that you and a few coyotes like you have got ears a mile long,' Radford said bitterly. 'But I'm goin' to print this editorial like I said, Curly. Now give me back that proof and get the hell outa here!'

Suddenly Radford's own shooting-iron was in his hand from the bench in front of him — but he was not quick enough. Curly flashed out his gun and fired from the hip. Radford hesitated for a long moment, red soaking across his shirt — then clawing at the proof-sheet and type on the bench he went reeling to the floor, the lead from the editorial clattering round him like hail.

'Uncle! Uncle!' Ann flung herself down beside him, tugged at his shoulders, hot tears streaming down her distraught face.

'Yellin' your head off ain't goin' to do yuh no good,' Curly observed, dropping the blackened remains of the proof-sheet he had now set alight to the floor, and grinding it under his heel.

Then he moved forward and roughly dragged the girl to her feet.

'An' if yuh try and talk too much about this it'll be too bad for yuh, see? Your uncle was goin' to shoot first; I had to shoot him in self-defence. An' that's what the law'll say.'

'Mark Grayson's law, yes!' Ann gritted back at him. 'What law there is here is crooked and rotten, like the whole town.'

'Best thing yuh can do is get movin', whilst I cleans things up in here. I'll report everythin' to the sheriff and tell him just what happened — my version, anyway!' Curly sneered, and shoved her fiercely towards the doorway. 'An' if yuh try 'n leave town to get help from Red Gap it won't do yuh any good. I'm warnin' yuh on that. Now get out.'

He yanked the door open and thrust her outside with such force she overbalanced and collapsed in the baking dust.

Eyes blurred with tears she scrambled up again and stood staring back helplessly at the print shop. Then at last she turned and went off slowly down the street.

It had happened just as her uncle had expected it would — but sooner. Help! That she had got to have . . .

Her mind still spinning with the shock of events, she tried to focus on what she should do next. It was no good going to the sheriff. As Grayson's friend, she knew he would accept Curly's twisted version of events.

And if she rode and told her father now, he was bound to come charging into town with Kenyon and the boys to avenge his brother-in-law's killing. That could lead to a mass slaughter!

The thought of her father being killed as well as her uncle made her shudder. Of course, he'd have to know what had happened, and soon, but that could wait. Her poor uncle Gil was already beyond all help . . .

Her rounded chin set firmly as she recalled the instructions her uncle had given her. Yes, carrying out his last wishes had to be her first priority.

Abruptly she made up her mind. She mounted on her mousy-coloured dun, and raced out of the arid waste of Dry Acres to the rising land beyond.

She rode hard, the wind drying the

tears on her face, the sturdy horse kicking up the hellish dust behind.

Five miles to the south of Dry Acres Ann drew rein, grasped the saddle horn and looked about her. Just here the landscape was chiefly barren mountain foothills, except for one massive oak leaning oddly sideways through the incessant pressure of the mountain winds.

Beyond it lay the trail that led to the neighbouring town of Red Gap, which Mitchell had warned her not to try reaching.

Ann dismounted quickly, began to unfasten the red kerchief from about her throat, and hurried towards the tree.

When she came back to her horse another horse was beside it, and both of them were nibbling at sparse grass roots.

'Evenin', Miss Ann!'

The girl swung, her eyes hard and suspicious in the dimming light. Very faintly she could descry the figure of

Curly Mitchell, the end of a cigarette pulsing redly as he drew on it.

'Yuh was spotted leavin' town,' he said evenly. 'Soon as I'd finished tellin' the sheriff my story, I came straight after yuh. Thought I told yuh to make no breaks for it,' he added grimly.

'You're not leavin' town, Miss Ann — them's the boss's orders. Get back on that horse!'

The girl hesitated, then: 'All right,' she said, surprisingly. 'I'll come back with you now.'

Curly gave a grunt of approval. What he failed to notice was that she was smiling tightly to herself as she swung easily into the saddle. As she set off at a steady jog down the trail to Dry Acres Curly caught up with her.

'Glad you're bein' sensible, Miss Ann. I wouldn't have liked to have shot yuh — but if you'd gone on I'd have *had* to.'

'It wouldn't make no odds with you whom you shot!' the girl retorted.

'Yuh got me wrong, ma'am. I only

shoot on orders or to save myself. Anyway, the boss told me to watch yuh because he'd got it figured that you'd likely make a break for it . . . An' he wants to see yuh, too.'

'See me?' Ann frowned.

'That's what he said. Yuh'd best do as he asks.'

Ann said no more until they had returned to Dry Acres. It was early evening now, and the Black Slipper saloon was rapidly filling up.

Outside the saloon Ann and Curly tied their horses to the boardwalk rail and entered through the batwings. Curly pushed a way through the throng, and went up the stairs at one side of the room, one arm holding the girl's arm.

Reaching Grayson's private office door he knocked and opened it without being asked.

'Here she is, chief,' Curly announced.

'Okay. Y'can get out.'

Curly went and Ann was left studying the man at the roll-top desk.

He was a familiar enough figure to her, but every time she saw him she felt that same fascinated revulsion. Mark Grayson was a well-built man, dressed carefully in black, with a fancy waist-coat and shoestring bow dangling down an expanse of white shirt.

His head, unusually large, sported a tangled mass of dark-brown curly hair. This, combined with a heavy nose and powerful mouth, gave him some claim to handsomeness, only it was snatched away again by the icy coldness of the light-blue eyes. There was no compassion in those eyes, no hint of human kindliness.

'Sorry about your uncle, Miss Ann,' Grayson said, angling round and motioning to a chair. 'He shouldn't have been so quick on the draw. I'd sort of like to help you out.'

'*You* help me?' Ann echoed in scorn, seating herself. 'You've got a damned nerve, haven't you?'

'Yeah — why not? Though your uncle had queer ideas on newspaper editin''

I'm not holding anythin' against you personally. You're different stuff — an' a swell looker too. You've only got to be sensible, see things the way I see 'em, and you and me can go a long ways in this town — or any other town.'

Ann was silent, acutely aware that another of her uncle's predictions had come true. He had said Grayson had a soft spot for her.

Was it sensible to openly revile him, as her instincts cried out for her to do, or was there more chance of learning something by pretending to go along with him? Some bit of evidence?

Perhaps some clue, which had vanished from before her eyes when she had been thrown out of the print shop and lost all chance of seeing the editorial her uncle had written, before Curly had dismantled the type? Perhaps his liking for her could prove to be his Achilles heel . . .

'Naturally,' Grayson went on, shrugging, 'you can't go on editin' that paper. I've taken over the offices myself and will put them to some other use. And, I'll be happy to pay you for it — and handsomely. Radford not bein' married I guess you'll be inheritin' his estate . . . ' he hesitated, looking at the girl to see how she was taking the line he was giving her.

Ann forced back the angry retort that had sprang to mind. She compressed her lips, and carefully controlled her voice before she replied:

'Anything else?'

Grayson looked surprised, then pleased. 'Well, naturally I won't be able to pay until the conveyance is sorted out. That will take time, of course, while we get it all tied up nice an' legal. But I really want to help you, Ann . . . ' he smiled expansively, revealing strong teeth that somehow reminded Ann of a shark. She repressed a shudder.

Grayson seemed to be leading up to something — but what?

'It's no secret in town that you and your old man won't be makin' no fortune with those half-starved animals of yours at the Roaring G yonder.'

'But for you they wouldn't be half-starved!' Ann retorted, unable to disguise her real feelings any longer. 'We had a good ranch until you diverted the watercourse! And we wouldn't be so short of money either, if it wasn't for paying the increased taxes that your friend the mayor's started imposing on homesteaders — '

'I had to teach the menfolk in your family a lesson, Miss Ann, an' it was your father's own fault that he never learned it. All he had to do to get his water back was publish a retraction of the things he said about me, which your uncle published in his paper when I first came here . . . ' Grayson stretched out his legs and contemplated his carefully polished boots.

'As I was sayin', you need financial help, until I fix the money for your print shop. You can sing, if you like. In my saloon.'

Ann gave a start. So this was why

Grayson had sent for her. She thought swiftly before dismissing the idea out of hand.

The only singing she had ever done had been in the church choir, before Mark Grayson had turned the place into the town's livery stable especially for his own favoured guests.

'You've got a swell voice,' Grayson added, eyeing her lasciviously. 'I've heard it. With the right dress' — and he sized up her slender figure in the blue Levis and check shirt — 'you'd be a cinch for the Black Slipper. But,' he shrugged, 'if you don't want the job, then . . . '

Ann reflected swiftly. Her father needed money to prevent the possible foreclosure of his ranch. Already in the town, more than one rancher had had to hand over the deeds of his property to Mayor Binalt in lieu of unpaid taxes.

'It's a hard world, Miss Ann — if you go against it.' Grayson smiled broadly, as the girl still hesitated. 'I'll pay you really well to work for me. A beautiful woman like you would be a big attraction in here.'

'And why are you so anxious to put a good thing in my way?'

'I've my reasons; and I don't want to see you hard put to it while we fix up the sale of the print shop. Besides, deep down, I'm hopin' you an' me'll see eye to eye one day.'

Ann considered for a long moment. Fight him and be crushed? Go with him and maybe help her own plans to avenge her uncle along? Her firm little chin tautened.

'All right, Mr Grayson.' She gave a shrug. 'But I can't start for a few days. I've got to tell my father his brother-in-law's dead, and arrange the funeral . . . '

'Naturally!' Grayson's voice was conciliatory. 'I know you were fond of your uncle, and I guess you'll need time to grieve a little. But shall we say next Monday?'

'All right,' Ann said. 'I'll start next week. But don't expect too many favours. Even if I have lost everything else I've still got my self-respect.'

★ ★ ★

It was the Monday evening following the weekend in which Gil Dalman had been buried at the family plot on the Roaring G. It had been extremely difficult for Ann's father to accept the situation, and go along with Ann's plan, but finally he had reluctantly acquiesced — but only after the girl had told him the full details of his brother's last wishes.

Even so, when he had ridden into town with Ginger to collect his brother's body from the sheriff's office where Curly had taken it, he had confronted Binalt.

Angrily, he had related Ann's version of what had really happened in the newspaper offfices. Binalt had appeared to listen sympathetically, only to tell Dalman that without an independent witness, as the law prescribed, he was unable to arrest Curly.

The time was nearing ten o'clock, and Grayson's Black Slipper saloon was pretty crowded as Ann, attired in a low-cut sequinned dress which the big fellow had rustled up from somewhere, sang in a fairly musical contralto to the accompaniment of 'Keys' Morgan's piano playing.

Her eyes went over the poker-layouts and pool-tables, beyond them to where the cowpunchers of Dry Acres and a sprinkling of people from neighbouring towns — news of the latest attraction had spread fast — sat at their drinks or played cards, and further still to the bar where Grayson's manager and bar-tender, Andy Parker, was wiping the drink-slopped counter.

As she sang over the hubbub Ann wondered on many things. Chiefly she thought of her uncle, lying in his grave alongside that of his sister, her mother, in the pastures of the Roaring G.

She wondered too if she and her father would ever be paid for the print shop; and particularly she wondered about their future. She was not here for singing only: there were other reasons. And she could not leave Dry Acres without chancing a bullet in her back . . .

Then her eyes turned to the distant batwings as they swung inwards and outwards behind a tall figure, his dark-blue shirt and trousers covered with the dust of his ride. Twin guns slapped his thighs as he walked over to the bar and cuffed up his black sombrero.

The newcomer ordered his drink and then turned so that Ann could see his face. It was lean and brown with a strong jaw and light-coloured eyes. Ann went on singing, but now she smiled a little too.

The stranger finished his drink and as Ann had appraised him over the smoke of cheroots and cigarettes so he had appraised her. He glanced at the barman.

'Who's the singer?' he asked briefly,

and his voice had an education uncommon in Dry Acres.

'Gal by the name o' Ann Dalman,' Parker answered. 'If you've any ideas, feller, forget 'em! She's the boss's especial property.'

'Yeah!' The stranger rubbed his sharp jaw pensively; then he said, 'Talkin' of the boss I want a word with him. Mark Grayson, isn't it?'

'Who'd be wantin' him?' Parker asked suspiciously.

'He wouldn't know me — but you can tell him the name's Blake Carson. And you can also tell him it's urgent.'

The bartender left his post for a moment or two, then came back and nodded to a rear door.

'The boss'll see you. Go on in.'

Blake Carson nodded and strolled easily to the nearby doorway, passed inside and stood facing Grayson as he worked at his desk.

'Howdy,' Grayson greeted eventually, looking up. 'What c'n I do for you, stranger?'

'Well, it's this way . . . ' Blake Carson swung a chair round and sat on it so that his elbows rested on the back.

'Without offence, it seems to me you ain't so particular what kind of fellers you have working for you. I thought you might use me. I had to get out of Three Gap Basin — made it too hot for myself.'

'Doing what?' Grayson asked round his cheroot.

Carson unfastened his shirt pocket and tossed two new-looking dollar bills down on the desk.

'Because of those,' he explained. 'My own handiwork.'

Grayson picked them up, compared them with one of his own dollar bills, held them to the light. The newcomer watched him impassively. At last Grayson raised an eyebrow.

'You mean you can turn out work like this?'

'If I'm allowed to fix my own presses, I can. I thought you an' me might do a deal.'

'With a guy who can duplicate dollars as good as this I'm willing,' Grayson said. 'And if you're plannin' some kind of a double-cross I know how to take care o' that, too. You won't be cramped here, stranger, and I reckon the best place you can have is the old *Gazette* print shop. The old feller who ran it opened his mouth too wide.'

'Print shop?' Carson considered, then nodded slowly. 'Okay, I know a bit about presses and printing as those bills show. I guess I'll take it on. And if anybody starts gunnin' for me, what happens?'

'I'll take care of that,' Grayson said. 'You look after me an' do as I say and you'll be around to tell about it. If you don't . . . ' He stopped, then grinned.

'Well, I'll tell you the *Gazette*'s layout and you can start in to hammer out some legitimate news as a cover-up for your homework. The paper isn't hard to handle: I'll pay you what I think you're worth after a week's trial.'

2

In a week the easy-going stranger had justified Grayson's faith in him by running the paper exactly as ordered and asking no questions.

A feature article on the new singing attraction at the Black Slipper — which had increased takings considerably — pleased Grayson especially. Carson had one helper, Curly Mitchell, and he had no tales to tell back to the boss. In fact it seemed as if Carson was all he claimed to be — a wanderer with a gift for forgery.

Ann saw him once or twice, but in public she never took any notice of him, nor he of her. He spent his time printing the *Gazette* and casting what he called the initial drawings for his dollar-bill forgeries — and Ann continued to sing. There was nothing to indicate what might happen next.

By degrees Carson was considered to be on the level from the point of view of Grayson and his cohorts, and therefore a prospective asset for the town's governing clique.

'One thing I don't understand,' Carson remarked pensively as he and Curly left the *Gazette* print shop late one night. 'Why does everybody here lie down and do just what the big fellow says? Not that I've any kicks, but I can't help wondering.'

'Ain't much choice when he's the only law an' order,' Curly answered, grinning.

'That's somethin' I don't quite get. What about Binalt? He's the town's mayor and sheriff. How come he seems to turn a blind eye to everythin'? Is he on a kickback?'

Curly shrugged. 'I wouldn't know. None o' my business, I reckon — nor yourn! And as for those who don't like his brand o' law an' order . . . ' He slapped his gun holster. 'Always a present waitin' for 'em.'

Carson considered as they walked along. 'I s'pose we're fighting on the right side, Curly? The boss knows what he's doin'? The law can't clamp down on him from other directions? Because he's gotten away with it so far in this dump it doesn't say he'll go on doin' it, does it?'

'Far as I know everythin's tied up nice an' legal,' Curly answered. 'He's taken watercourses for his own use, exchanged cattle, traded with neighbourin' towns. The whole dope about him's locked up in that safe of his in his office.' Curly scratched his chin, and went on:

'Sometimes I wish I could see inside that safe properly. Reckon there'd be plenty of interestin' stuff in it. I once heard a sorta rumour that Grayson is wanted in quite a few towns, an' I think old man Gil Radford knew that too. Be a reward from the Rangers mebby . . .'

Carson glanced at Curly's shifty face and grinned.

'Information worth printin', huh? In the *Gazette*?'

'Yeah — but not if you want to go on breathin', feller!' Curly laughed harshly.

They had come to the end of the street on the way to the bunkhouse, but Carson stopped and stood gazing at the dark expanse of Dalman's Roaring G ranch. Then he glanced at Curly.

'That Dalman gal in the Black Slipper has given me the brush-off once or twice,' he confided. 'I didn't quite like it. What say that frozen piece's spread catches fire accidentally while she's singing?'

Curly grinned. Such sport had never occurred to him. He was remembering how Ann never missed a chance to slight and try to humiliate him, in front of others whenever their paths crossed in the town. The fact that his having murdered her uncle might have something to do with it never entered his mind. Wouldn't it just serve that frigid dame right!

'Mebby teach her a lesson,' Carson

added. 'She'll have no place to go. Get busy and fire the dump. I'll keep a watch.'

Curly nodded and hurried forward into the gloom. Carson watched him go, took a long look on every side of him, then backed away into the darkness. In a moment or two the first flare of fire spurted in a crackling roar to the night sky.

The sun-scorched timber flared avidly, sending a cloud of drifting sparks towards the town on the mountain breeze.

Carson still waited, now hidden in the shadows of the buildings. He saw Curly come back and look for him — and then look round in some alarm at the fury of the fire he had started.

It was spreading with diabolical speed. Soon the whole town would be threatened . . .

There were voices as Carson stood there, then the sound of running feet and horses as the inhabitants of Dry Acres came out to see what was wrong.

Presently Grayson himself arrived.

'What goddamned fool started this?' he yelled. Then, as he caught sight of his henchman:

'Hey, Curly, you know anythin' about this?'

'It was that guy Carson,' Curly said, anxious to divert the blame. 'I was too late to stop him. He said somethin' about it teachin' Miss Ann a lesson — '

'Where is he now?' Grayson snapped, suppressed fury in his voice.

'Dunno. Ran off some place, I guess. Scared mebby of the way this fire's spread — '

'The *whole town*'s goin' to catch fire if we don't stop this!' Grayson swung round, his brain working quickly. 'Hey, you men — get some dynamite, quick! Blow up that watercourse dam on the hillside there. The pent-up water will rush down here and help us . . . '

And while Grayson was shouting instructions outside the town, Carson was gliding into the empty reaches of the Black Slipper. Only a blonde girl with a pale face was present. She hurried over and caught his arm.

'Did — did it work?' she asked breathlessly.

'Yeah. Trust a fire in this climate! Come in here.' He caught her arm and led her into Grayson's office, then he closed the door carefully.

'From what Curly's been telling me I reckon all the evidence we need is in that safe,' he said. 'Just as I figured it would be. If I can put it before the right authority in Caradoc City he's finished.'

'And if he finds us?' Ann asked anxiously. Then she looked up at the sudden sound of the distant concussion of exploding dynamite.

'We'll risk it. The fire will keep him busy.' Carson went on one knee before the safe and glanced up at the girl.

'Did you manage to get the combination?'

Ann handed over a slip of paper from her dress. 'Near as I could. He only opened it twice in my presence.' Ann gave a little shiver as she remembered the times when she had had to pretend to be friendly with Grayson, alone in his office. She didn't want to go through anything like that again.

Carson studied the numbers intently and fingered the dial gently.

'I only wish you'd come before they got my uncle, Blake,' the girl muttered, watching him. 'He'd probably be alive now . . .'

'Mebby. Anyway, that signal of a knotted red kerchief you left on the tree was enough. I always told your uncle I'd help him out if ever I could since he once tried to save my father out in the desert. The least a son can do for his old man's memory. Thanks for helping since I arrived here . . .'

'The ranch wanted burning down anyway. Dad had Ginger move all valuable stuff out, and cattle too . . .'

Ann broke off as Carson suddenly gave a pleased grunt as he found the combination. The safe door swung open. He snatched up and examined the documents inside, then he glanced up with a start as the office window smashed in abruptly. Grayson was framed in the window, his gun levelled menacingly.

'Not so fast, Carson!' he snapped, elbowing the remaining glass out of the way and stepping into the office from the landing outside.

'Curly put me wise to your probable intentions. The law says I can kill a trespasser, remember. Put your guns on the floor!'

Slowly, his eyes narrowed, Carson unfastened his belt and let it clatter round his feet. Then with the swiftness of a panther he lashed up his right fist.

It struck Grayson on the chin as his gun exploded and sent him crashing with such force against the office door the catch snapped, precipitating him down the short flight of stairs and into the saloon.

Instantly Carson was after him. A few of the Dry Acres inhabitants were standing near the batwings now, watching. Outside the watercourse had mastered the danger of town-wide fire . . .

Then came Curly, sneaking silently up with levelled six-shooter. He raised it and sighted Carson's back — but before he could fire a bullet whanged from the office doorway.

Ann Dalman stood there, the smoke of one of Carson's guns wafting round her face.

Grayson thrust out a desperate hand to seize the gun Curly had dropped, just as the henchman reeled to the floor, there to sprawl unmoving. Just as Gil Dalman had done.

Curly failed to appreciate the irony: he was dead before he hit the floor. Grayson got the gun in his fingers, turned the muzzle on the back of the man hammering his face — but just as he pulled the trigger, Carson drew himself back in order to better deliver a knockout blow. He stopped with retracted arm as Grayson sagged weakly under the explosion of the gun. He himself had got the bullet.

Slowly Carson got up, rubbing a sleeve across his face. He gazed round on the cowpunchers, as Ann, white-faced and trembling slightly, came over to him.

She buried her face in his chest and he put an arm about her shoulders.

'Those of you who followed Grayson would be best advised to quit town and hit the trail,' he announced curtly, looking about him. 'I intend to call in a marshal to this town.'

There was a shifting and stirring as the cohorts of the dead Grayson vanished through the batwings. Those who remained — the honest folk of the town — gave an ironic cheer.

'Nice goin', son!' one old-timer remarked. 'This town'll smell a whole lot sweeter from now on!' There were murmurs of assent from the rest of the assembled population.

Carson grinned a little and turned to the girl, who, recovering, had gently disengaged herself from his arms, and now stood looking at him wonderingly.

'Quite recently, Ann, your uncle wrote to tell me that he believed he was near to proving that Grayson was really Mark Glanton, an outlaw whom the authorities have been trying to find for the last three years,' he explained.

'Evidently he *had* proved it, only to get shot for his pains, but beforehand he'd written me a letter arranging the kerchief signal in case of trouble. When I saw it — since I rode by that tree regularly, watching for it — I came here as soon as I could.'

'For which Dad and I are eternally grateful,' the girl smiled. 'Our ranch got burned down, but we got a watercourse in exchange! We should be able to rebuild . . . but one thing worries me,' she broke off uncertainly. 'I shot that man — '

'Curly? Don't worry: you only did that to save me. I can testify to that, and there were other witnesses here, too.

You've nothing to worry over, when I call in the law.'

'So you say. But Henry Binalt is the law around here,' Ann said, frowning. 'He's both the sheriff and mayor, and — '

'Too damned right, I am!' a gravelly voice snapped.

Carson and the girl turned as through the batwings came the scowling figure of Henry Binalt himself, a gun in his right hand. Behind him, also armed, came the tall figure of Brad Dugan, his deputy and right-hand man.

Binalt, to his credit, at least looked official. He was massively built, with thick, black wavy hair. His face, though now scowling, could look deceptively genial when it suited him.

'What the hell's been goin' on here?' Binalt demanded. 'My deputy and I just got back from checkin' on the fire when we heard shootin' . . . '

'You're too late, Sheriff,' the old-timer remarked, with a leathery grin.

'Someone's already done your job for yuh!'

'Yeah — as usual!' a puncher commented, grinning. Then his smile melted as Dugan fixed him with a baleful stare.

Binalt had caught sight of the sprawled corpses of Grayson and Curly, which the barkeep and a couple of helpers were commencing to drag from where they had fallen, towards one side of the room.

'My God! Grayson and Curly — shot dead!' He stood for a second, or two, his features working. It was hard to read his expression. It could have been surprise, rage — or even fear. His gun swung menacingly towards Carson.

'Reckon you'd better start explaining yourself, feller,' he grated. 'Grayson was an important member of this community, and whoever killed him is going to pay . . .'

Carson looked at Binalt without flinching. 'You need to get a few things straight, mayor or sheriff, whatever capacity you're supposed to be actin' in. For one thing — that guy isn't called Grayson! His *real* name was Mark Glanton, an outlaw wanted in half a dozen states . . . '

Binalt's eyes flickered. He was about to attempt to rebut the assertion, then catching sight of the sea of uncompromising faces from the people now encircling them, with more crowding through the batwings, he thought better of it. He compressed his lips, and shrugged.

'Keep talkin'!' he snapped.

'For another,' Carson said, 'nobody killed him — he shot himself, as everyone here will testify. And his cohort lying there is a murderer, who was shot whilst attempting to add to his tally.'

Binalt seemed to be thinking swiftly. The naked hostility — and evident support from the assembled towns-people for what Carson was saying — was palpable.

'Naturally, if what you say is true,

stranger, then that sure makes a difference.' He forced a conciliatory note into his voice. 'And as sheriff and mayor, it'll be my duty to investigate and get to the bottom of this.'

Carson shook his head, smiling thinly. 'I don't think so, Binalt. I intend using the telegraph to call in a marshal from Caradoc City. Glanton was wanted in several states, and that lifts it outside of your local jurisdiction. The Texas Rangers will be interested, too — and especially in the documents I found in the safe upstairs. I intend doing my explainin' to them . . . ' he paused, looking round on the assembly, and then at the tight-lipped Binalt.

'Come to think of it,' he added, 'I might not be the only one with some explainin' to do.'

'What do you mean by that remark?' Binalt said, striving to control himself.

'Nothing much — 'cept that Glanton was able not only to hide his identity, but to carry on his criminal activities

— right under your nose! Funny that, ain't it?'

★ ★ ★

It was late in the evening when Carson took his leave of Ann Dalman and her father, having escorted the girl to Ma Falkner's boarding-house, where her father had booked rooms in the town until the fire-damaged Roaring G ranch could be rebuilt.

'I'm repeatin' my offer, son,' Old Man Dalman said, as Carson unhitched his mount from the tie rail outside. 'I'll be needin' assistance to help me get the ranch goin' again. I'm willin' to make you a partner.' He looked at his daughter, and smiled at the girl's expression as she looked intently at Carson swinging into the saddle. 'An' I'm sure Ann would make you mighty welcome . . .'

'Thanks, Mr Dalman. I really appreciate your offer, but I guess I already have my own business in Red Gap. I'm a carpenter and timber-merchant there ... But, say, I've been thinkin' ... ' He smiled down at Ann, who was looking acutely disappointed, 'I could do worse than transfer my business to Dry Acres,' Carson mused. 'Seems to me that in the aftermath of that fire, I might be able to pick up more than a little business in this town ... '

'You're danged right there, son.' Dalman chuckled.

' . . . and perhaps I could help out on your ranch in my spare time,' Carson finished. 'That's if it'd be all right with you, Miss Ann?'

'Of course.' The girl was smiling now. 'There's nothing I'd like better. But there's one thing that's been bothering me.'

'What's that?' Carson asked.

'Those forged dollar notes! Wherever did you get them?'

Carson laughed. 'Those! Why, bless your heart, they were straight out of the previous day's takings at my timber store. Two of the best Uncle Sam ever made!'

3

To Henry Binalt, the past few weeks had been a time of uncertainty and mounting strain. Life in Dry Acres had once been extremely satisfying — but that had been before the arrival of Blake Carson.

Now Binalt faced an uncertain future, and just at a time when he could least afford it. That was the most damnable aspect of the whole business! There was a massive fortune within his grasp, and he had no intention of letting it elude him.

Before Carson had interfered, Binalt had, using the late Mark Glanton as a front man, maintained a stranglehold on the homesteaders. Now he was losing that grip. The change had started in a small way, but had now grown into a positive cloud, so dense indeed that it definitely threatened him with losing the approaching election.

'No, Brad, I don't like it,' he muttered. 'I don't like it a damned bit!'

Brad Dugan did not make any comment. He was noted for not appearing to show any emotions — a gift that with the coming of Binalt had raised him from the lowly status of cowpuncher to being the mayor and sheriff's chief confidant. Binalt liked Dugan's aim with a gun and the implacable manner in which he could take care of incidents.

At the moment Dugan was half-lounging against the roll-top desk in the mayoral office, studying the big fellow as he stood at the open window gazing out into the sun-drenched main street of the little town . . . All other considerations apart, Henry Binalt could not help looking the part.

Impressively built, and handsome after a fashion, he could appear avuncular when he wanted. He invariably dressed in a black suit and, when outside, a large black sombrero. One of his perpetual cheroots was now smouldering between his jutting lips and the blaze of sunlight caught the thick, dark oily waves of his hair.

'If Carson goes on much longer like this he's likely to get the people around to his way of thinking, and that wouldn't do me much good . . . ' Binalt spoke half to himself and then turned to aim a dark-eyed glance at his henchman. 'He's already somethin' of a local hero after the way he put one over on Glanton.'

'I reckon you ain't all that much call to get all het up over that jigger, boss,' Brad Dugan answered, shrugging. 'He says a lot, and says it nicely, but the folks around here still know who's boss.'

As he spoke he lounged over to the open window and gazed through it. A little further down the main street, standing on a buckboard and waving his arms to emphasize his meaning, was Blake Carson, the rival candidate for election — an animated, dark-haired figure of youthful dynamism.

In the few short weeks since he had cleaned out Glanton, and come to live in the town, Blake Carson had risen from his almost obscure position as a timber-merchant and carpenter in the neighbouring town of Red Gap, to one of Dry Acres' most prominent citizens. More, he was becoming seen as a champion of the oppressed.

Around him at this very moment, crowding into the dusty street, some mounted on horseback and leaning on their saddle horns as they listened, others lounging against the tie rails edging the boardwalks, was quite a large gathering.

That he was taking time out from his timber store further down the street did not worry Blake Carson. Morning or evening, when the greatest number of people were about, were the periods he usually chose for his canvassing.

'To hear that guy shootin' his face, boss, you'd think honesty were the best policy,' Brad Dugan remarked with a sour grin. 'Hear what he's sayin'? He sure wants shuttin' up.'

In snatches Blake Carson's voice came on the still air.

' . . . and what does Binalt do for you folks whilst he is in office? Nothing! Nothing, I tell you! With taxes and restrictions he's got the lot of you hog tied. You know you're being short-changed but you don't do anything about it because you're scared. Just as you were once scared of Mark Grayson — alias the outlaw, Mark Glanton.'

There was a murmur in the crowd at the name of the former oppressor whom Carson had removed.

'I can alter all that. Elect me and you'll soon see a difference. I . . . '

Henry Binalt turned away from the window in disgust, tugged his cheroot from his mouth and stood contemplating it.

'I can take care of him, boss, if you want me to,' Dugan reminded him, and his lean hands strayed to the walnut butts of the .45s low down on his thighs.

'No, not that,' Binalt said, throwing himself in the swivel-chair before the desk and pondering.

'To shoot the chief contestant in an election would make a smell that would reach the authorities in Caradoc City, and bring that damned marshal back here again. A second such investigation and I might find myself attending a necktie party in double-quick time. I've got to be careful . . . '

'Why, boss?'

'Because I was only chosen as mayor and sheriff by a majority of votes given by the will of the people assembled at a special meeting in Glanton's saloon. He arranged the whole thing, including free drinks and intimidation to ensure the vote went my way. Glanton was damned useful to me, whilst he lived. I had him in my pocket because I knew his real identity. He covered for me because I protected him and let him do more or less as he liked.' Binalt made an irritated gesture.

'We ran the town between us. It was the perfect set-up until that damned Carson wiped out Glanton. The whole election thing was barely legal. I took no oath as sheriff . . . ' he scowled at Dugan, who had reverted to his habitual impassivity.

'Why the hell else do you think I agreed to this damned new election in the first place?' Binalt went on. 'It was to divert the suspicions of that marshal, and make myself secure. To unsettle my arrangements by a murder now would be just hollering out loud for trouble. And as for your complacency, Dugan, you've no sense of herd instinct. You can push the folks so far — but not too far.'

He got up from the swivel-chair and paced the office, puffing furiously at his cheroot.

'I've never shown open hostility and that's why the folks half-believe what I tell 'em. Otherwise I'd never have held down my position, even with Glanton's help. One of 'em would have got me for certain.'

Dugan ran a finger pensively along his bony jaw.

'Look boss, mebby it's none o' my business, but just why *did* you start soaking these homesteaders with big taxes? You started just before Glanton got wiped out, and have continued to do it afterwards. I can't figure out the angle. Y'make it so's they can't pay for their ranches and homes any more an' then you buy their properties up. Why? Or is that none o' my business?'

'That's right, it's none of your business,' Binalt told him, and added a grim glance. 'You stick to doin' as you're told and leave the thinkin' to me.'

He got up again and paced the room restlessly.

'Just the same I've got to think of *something*. The way things are going Carson might even get away with it ... *What the* ... ?' Binalt broke off with a start of surprise.

54

Pandemonium and revolver shots had suddenly broken loose in the main street outside his office.

Men were running, women were diving for the comparative safety of the ramshackle bunkhouses and stores, and Blake Carson had flung himself flat in the buckboard.

Again, in quick succession, three more revolver shots exploded in the hot morning air, then the originator of the upheaval became mistily apparent in a cloud of blinding dust — a lone horseman, masked with a black neckerchief, his agile figure clothed in a dusty black shirt, tight pants, and a black Stetson.

'I think I recognize that jigger, boss,' Dugan breathed, with a fascinated stare.

'I reckon that'll be Jeff Oakroyd, the outlaw! There's ten thousand dollars offered for him if we're to believe them reward-dodgers.'

Binalt did not answer. His cheroot at an angle he watched the hurtling gunman as the horse, a pinto, bore him down the street.

The rider stopped and dismounted suddenly, tying the horse's reins to the hitch rail of the Black Slipper saloon — now another of Binalt's money-making enterprises — and then with gun in hand he strode through the batwings and vanished. The purpose of his visit to town was, apparently, to slake his thirst with liquor.

'You're right, Brad,' Binalt breathed. 'It's Oakroyd all right — and that gives me an idea!'

The lanky gunhawk did not ask what it was because he knew he would get no answer. Binalt was never free with information. He followed his boss to the office door and then stopped as Binalt glanced at him.

'Stick around here, Brad; I'm attendin' to this myself.'

'OK, but you're stickin' your chin out, boss. That jigger's likely to blow the dust from under yuh.'

'Shut up,' Binalt answered briefly,

and, snatching down his hat from the peg, he jammed it on his head and left the office.

Both hands resting lightly on the twin .38s he carried he walked across the street slowly towards the Black Slipper. The people were emerging again now from their hiding-places, watching Binalt's progress with intent interest.

Here, Binalt reflected, was good psychology — far better than the vapourings of young Carson. Here was courage in action — the mayor-sheriff going personally to try and capture the biggest desperado in the territory . . .

That, on the face of it, was how it looked — even to Blake Carson himself who was now standing up again on the buckboard, watching intently.

With measured strides Binalt finished the journey across the street, strode up the three steps to the boardwalk outside the saloon, then yanked out both his guns and pushed the batwing doors open with them.

As he had expected, the saloon beyond was gloomy and untidy. It was in the mornings that the place was cleaned up in readiness for the noon and evening rush. But despite the dim light Jeff Oakroyd was visible lounging against the bar-counter, one revolver pointing steadily at the aproned figure of Andy Parker, who, until this had happened, had been busily mopping the floor.

The instant the batwings were pushed open Oakroyd's left-hand gun swung round on the advancing figure of Binalt.

'Drop them guns!' ordered a hard voice behind the neckerchief mask.

Binalt did not drop his guns. Instead he paused, standing just within the saloon looking at his manager.

'Get moving, Andy,' he ordered. 'Go on — get outa here.'

An order from the mayor and sheriff was an order, and Andy obeyed it, expecting to get a slug in his back from the thirsty bandit as he did so. But

Oakroyd did not fire. He was apparently so astonished at the command that he held his fire and waited to see what happened next.

Then, when the frightened Andy had skedaddled beyond the batwings into the street, the bandit turned gently and, resting his elbows backwards on the bar-counter, levelled both his guns at the slowly advancing Binalt.

'Mebby yuh didn't get my meanin',' he said slowly. 'I said *drop* 'em! I ain't a-talkin' just for the hell of it.'

A bullet whanged and took Binalt's black sombrero clean off his head. Stolid, grim-faced, he dropped his twin guns to the floor with a clatter.

'That sure is better,' Oakroyd observed. He lifted the pointed base of his neckerchief mask, swallowed his drink, then let the neckerchief drop back into position.

Cold, light-blue eyes, the only feature of his face visible, stared at Binalt from under the brim of the shabby black Stetson.

'Got your gall, ain't yuh?' he demanded. 'Only my good nature's a-stoppin' me blowin' your brains out right this minute.' Oakroyd paused as he again lifted his kerchief with the barrel of his gun, and took another drink.

'Since you got rid of that barkeep before I could question him, *you* had better answer me,' Oakroyd continued, his voice taut. 'Where the hell is Mark Grayson? This is his joint, ain't it?'

'Actually, it's mine now,' Binalt answered. Then he made his play: 'I took it over after Mark *Glanton* was killed . . . ' Binalt paused tensely, waiting to see the effect of his words.

Oakroyd straightened up, his eyes glinting dangerously. Obviously, he had known about the alias, and the news of Glanton's death had come as a profound shock to him.

'Mark Glanton — *dead*?' There was sheer disbelief in his voice. Then he raised his gun level with Binalt's tense face.

'Better talk fast, if you want to go on livin' . . . How did he die? Who killed him?'

'It wasn't me,' Binalt said hastily as Oakroyd's finger tightened on the trigger. 'I didn't see the killin' myself, but Mark Glanton got caught up in a fight, right here in this saloon, about a month ago. He was fightin' a young guy called Blake Carson. His gun went off and Glanton took the bullet.' Binalt hesitated, licking his lips nervously.

As Oakroyd lowered the gun slightly, Binalt quickly outlined subsequent events.

'Hell an' damnation!' Oakroyd muttered. 'Glanton an' me used to ride together years ago, afore thing's got too hot, an' we had to split up. I heard he had settled in Dry Acres under a false monicker, and figured it would be a good place to hide out awhile — ' Oakroyd broke off, scowling at Binalt. 'Just who is this damned Carson guy? Is he still around?' he demanded.

'He's a do-gooder, and he's recently

moved into the town. Somehow he'd found out about Glanton, and made it his business to bring him down — '

'An' I'm makin' it *my* business right now to bring *him* down!' Oakroyd roared, slamming his emptied glass down on the bar so hard that it shattered. 'Glanton and I went way back . . . '

'I can help you,' Binalt said quietly. Inwardly he was elated at how events were playing into his hands.

'What the hell are yuh talking about?'

'I knew I took my life in my hands coming here to speak to Jeff Oakroyd,' Binalt hurried on, stopping beside the bar-counter, 'but I did it for a reason. First, though I'm sheriff and mayor of this town, I've no wish to capture you. That's up to the marshals: if they can't do it why in heck should I sweat myself in tryin'?'

Oakroyd tipped the whiskey bottle into another glass and held his left-hand gun steady on a line with Binalt's capacious stomach.

'Then what *do* yuh want?' Oakroyd demanded suspiciously. 'You'd better make it good, otherwise . . . '

'I'll get straight to the point,' Binalt said. 'I'm willing to pay you five thousand dollars in cash if you'll do a job for me — twenty-five hundred now and twenty-five hundred when you've finished. That'll keep you comfortable for a long time.'

Oakroyd gave a start, lowering his gun in sheer amazement. 'You're loco!' he declared bluntly.

'Not a bit.' Binalt regarded the shaded eyes calmly. 'I don't mind tellin' you I'm as much of an outlaw as you are — but I wouldn't be tellin' it to anybody *but* an outlaw. The only difference between us is that you were mug enough to pin a murder rap on yourself whereas I've steered clear of it — personally, that is. There's ten thousand dollars reward on you, dead or alive, and with a little ingenuity I could beat you and collect, but ten thousand dollars is low dice compared to what *I'm* after. If you're interested, I'll tell you what I want you to do . . . '

Oakroyd lifted the neckerchief slightly and downed another drink; then as he lowered the neckerchief back into place again he nodded.

'Sure I'm interested. Keep talkin'.'

'When you rode into town this morning you probably saw a young guy talking to the people in the main street? From a buckboard?'

'Yeah, sure I did. He was right in my path. I fired straight at him because I didn't like his face, but I reckon I missed.'

'You did,' Binalt agreed. 'Leastways he was healthy enough to watch me come in here after you. But you can still take care of him. I want him rubbed out — bushwhacked. Savvy?'

'Why?'

'That's my business. Anyway, *my* reasons don't matter — I reckon you've got reason enough of your own now . . . ' Binalt paused, smiling cynically.

'You mean . . . *that critter were Carson?*'

'That's right. Kind of a pity you missed him, wasn't it?' Binalt reflected. 'But I've got a plan for you to get rid of him. You'll have every chance tonight — '

'Just a minute,' Oakroyd said, still suspicious. 'If you'd wanted him dead before, and you're an outlaw like you say, surely you'd have some owl-hooters of your own who could do that? Why pick on me particularly?'

'I've a dozen gunmen I can pick on but they wouldn't have any freedom of movement and might be recognized. I don't want that.' Binalt smiled. 'When I came in here to ask you to do this job for me, I hadn't realized you had known Glanton. He was a good friend of mine, too; we were sort of partners in runnin' the town . . . '

'Then I guess it's your lucky day. Right now, Carson's as good as dead,' Oakroyd growled. 'An' I don't need any plan, neither. Just tell me where this guy hangs out, an' — '

'Hear me out,' Binalt insisted. 'There's no need for you to take a risk with Carson. What happened to Glanton shows you the kind of thing that might go wrong — '

'You sayin' I'm yeller?' Oakroyd snapped, swinging up his gun again.

'Of course not! I'm just wanting to make *sure* of things.' Binalt eased his collar. 'Listen: every evening, when the men and women are on their way to this saloon he starts making a speech from a buckboard, same as he does in the mornings. Or most mornings, leastways: sometimes he misses — but in the evening around nine he never fails. I want you to ride into town this evening at that time — same as you did this mornin' — and take care of him. If you take care of others as well that's your fun, but you must get *him*. He's a danger to my interests. It'll be dark at that time and you can make good your escape. It'll also cover up whatever movements I might make.'

'There ain't nothin' simpler, I reckon,' Oakroyd said, thinking. 'But what about that money?'

Binalt felt in his jacket and pulled out a wallet, aware as he did so that the gun had cocked warily again in case anything more dangerous might be produced.

With the wallet in his hand, Binalt glanced behind him at the batwings. So far none of the populace had ventured near enough to see what was going on in the saloon.

'Here you are,' Binalt said, pulling out the bills. 'Twenty-five hundred dollars . . . Count 'em and be sure.'

Oakroyd laboriously did so with one hand; the gun was still in the other. Finally he nodded and stuffed the notes into his shirt pocket.

'You talk my lingo, mister,' he said. 'But what about the rest o' it? How'd I collect?'

'Well, obviously you mustn't have any visible connection with me or the whole plan would be useless. Here's what I'll do. You've seen that big sycamore tree at the end of the main street — as you come along the trail from Caradoc?'

'Yeah, I saw it. What about it?'

'I'll leave the money there for you, in an envelope on the first branch. I'll be watching what you do, of course, and the moment I see you've got Carson — and I've satisfied myself that he's dead — I'll ride out and fix things up for you, apparently chasing after you. If you do your job all right you'll find the money.'

'I'd better,' Oakroyd observed grimly. 'I ain't a-worryin' over wipin' out this guy Carson because I've already two murder raps over my head — an' I won't mind addin' one more if you don't come across as you've promised. OK, feller, you're on. You'll see me around nine tonight.'

'And before you leave there's somethin' else,' Binalt said.

'What?' Oakroyd had levelled his guns preparatory to leaving the saloon and tackling whoever might be outside as he went to get his pinto.

'I want you to leave here at a run — just as though you've done somethin' to me. I shan't attempt anythin', but to be sure of it you can walk out backwards with your guns on me.'

'Just what I'm aimin' to do,' Oakroyd replied sourly, and began leaving the saloon in reverse as he spoke.

Nothing happened until the gunman had dodged back through the batwings, then Binalt threw himself flat on the floor, smothered himself in dirt, ruffled his hair and pulled his collar awry.

As he heard the noise of the outlaw's horse's hoofs receding up the street, and the growing murmur of excited voices nearing the saloon, he began to stagger most effectually to his feet.

Questions began to rain on him from the men and women who came surging in. A cowhand picked up the fallen guns and handed them back.

'Thanks,' Binalt said, looking shaken and brushing back his thick hair. 'I wasn't so smart as I thought, I reckon. I did my best to get Oakroyd, but he had the drop on me, and ordered me to drop my guns. Then he shot at me! Mebby you heard it? The bullet missed and went through my hat. The only way I could save my life was to lie still and pretend to be dead. Then he got away . . . '

A speech calculated to do untold good to his election prospects.

With no evidences to the contrary the simple people of Dry Acres believed it — the majority, anyway. Some, never trusting Henry Binalt in any case, glanced at each other, and at the back of the crowd Blake Carson compressed his lips.

He did not credit a word of it, but naturally he had not the least idea what else to think. He stood watching as, still straightening himself out, Binalt left the saloon and limped back across the street to his office.

Brad Dugan was waiting for him there, standing beside the window.

'Looks like you got yourself in bad,

boss,' he commented drily.

'That's how it's *meant* to look.' Binalt sat down at his desk, relaxed and then grinned. 'I fixed it, Brad! Carson won't bother us no more after tonight, an' we can keep our noses clean, too. With him out of the way the election result is a cinch. You'll see.'

4

Ingeniously though Henry Binalt had contrived his scheme to deflect all suspicion from himself, there were other events shaping themselves outside his sphere of influence.

They were centred chiefly in Parry Kelby, US marshal, who was riding the lone trail from Caradoc City to Dry Acres, at just the time Jeff Oakroyd was beating a hasty retreat from the Black Slipper.

Parry Kelby was getting tired. The sun was blazing hot and the horse and saddle were sweaty. Kelby was not particularly on the alert: there was no reason why he should be until he reached Dry Acres, so he contented himself with surveying the glory of the Arizona spring.

On every side of the lone trail the mountains rose, ridged and peaked and grey, except where there were the silver-white patches of the Apache plumes and the vivid scarlet of the mallows. The trail itself ran between vast fields of brittle-bush, stretching away like golden carpets, while out upon the mesa that he had left behind danced the endless yuccas — the Lord's Candles — stately in their eight-foot-high clusters of snowy blooms.

In fact, even to Parry Kelby, on business bent, it constituted a real effort not to be fascinated by the infinite variety of nature. It made the investigation of law-breaking and intrigue seem somehow repugnant — but it had to be done.

The investigation a month before by another marshal — Parry's colleague, Walt Standish — from Caradoc City, had pointed to the fact that things were not entirely as they should be in the little town of Dry Acres. That investigation had actually been into the affairs of the late saloon-owner, 'Mark Grayson', but Standish had picked up local gossip that maybe the mayor and sheriff was behaving in a way contrary to the rulings of the authorities. It was doubtful if in the strict interpretation of the law he was entitled to be either mayor or sheriff.

More than this was not known. However, since Henry Binalt had now offered a democratic election in the town, there might not even be *any* truth in the yarns anyway: that was what Parry Kelby was going to find out.

Within the hour Parry reckoned that he would be in Dry Acres and able to take shelter from the glaring sun. Despite his lassitude from the heat he rode erectly, a lean, gaunt man with a skin tanned deep reddish brown.

He held the horse's reins lightly, giving the beast its head, making no effort to urge it forward in a temperature ranging towards a hundred degrees Fahrenheit. Sternness was the chief aspect of Parry Kelby's features. Mouth, chin, and nose all contributed to this effect, though in the light-blue eyes a faintly humorous twinkle revealed where the real nature of the man sparkled behind the official exterior.

He turned his head abruptly, his eyes slitting in the glare. His ears had caught an unexpected sound in the quivering, searing silence — the distant hollow reverberation of a horse's hoofs as a single rider travelled at high speed. He halted his mount and gazed fixedly.

It was not long before he caught sight of the rider speeding on a small pinto amidst the white clusters of anenome carpeting the floor of a not very distant canyon. For about half a minute the rider was fully in sight, then the towering grey spurs of rock hid him.

'No man has any need to travel at that speed, and in that direction — off trail — if he's up to any good . . . ' Parry Kelby spoke half to himself, thinking. Then, his marshal's instincts aroused, he swung round his horse's head and started off at a brisk canter in the direction of the canyon.

In a moment or two he reached it, neck-reined his horse and went on at a jog-trot. Caution led him to lift his .45 from the right holster and keep it poised — just in case.

Ahead of him the canyon was narrow, a mighty split in the mountain range, dancing with heatwaves, the yellow primroses and whispering bells crouching into the meagre shadows of the implacable grey walls.

There was no trail from the hurrying horseman, or at least no trail an ordinary man would have been able to follow. But Parry was *not* an ordinary man: his observations were heightened by his training. A crushed flower here, an overturned stone there, the semicircular mark of a horse's hoof in baked earth — these were the visible signs which kept him going, alert for anything which might happen.

Nothing did, and he wondered if he was a fool for wasting time; then the realization that no sane man would lose himself in this grey, friendless waste of torturing heat without a very good reason kept him exploring.

Suddenly the canyon ended in sheer precipice.

Parry drew rein and looked about him. Above, the crags and buttresses of the mountains and the cobalt-blue sky; below, perhaps 200 feet, the surging of a deep river, a creek swollen by the spring rains from melting snows far up the heights.

'Lookin' for somebody?'

Parry twisted round in his saddle as the coarse voice reached him. He could not see who was speaking but apparently the man was behind a nearby spire of rock.

'Drop your guns an' get off that cayuse o' yourn,' the voice ordered curtly. 'An' be quick about it!'

Parry tightened his mouth and obeyed, tossed both his guns into the dust and then dismounted, hands raised. He obeyed a further command to walk forward twelve paces from his horse and then watched a lean, tall figure emerge from behind a nearby spur of rock, black neckerchief well up to his eyes.

As he came forward Parry studied him intently, and a cold grin broke his mouth. His gaze dropped momentarily to pointing .38s.

'Jeff Oakroyd, if I'm not mistaken,' he commented grimly. 'You probably came here to try and link up with your old outlaw associate Mark Glanton. I wondered if I'd ever run into you in my travels.'

'Well, yuh done it — an' it ain't a-goin' to do yuh a mite o' good. I know yuh, too: Kelby, ain't yuh? A stinkin' marshal! Just as well I watched yuh followin' me. I like it around here, see — nice an' safe up in these mountain caves, an' I don't intend to let no marshal interfere with my privacy.'

Parry said nothing. In fact, having satisfied himself that the aggressor was Jeff Oakroyd there was nothing more he *could* say. He had recognized him from the pictures of his masked face, hat, and general build, a description that had been circulated to all centres of authority throughout the state.

And in that case the position was dangerous. A desperado like Jeff Oakroyd would not be particularly friendly towards a marshal.

'The fact that somethin' is a-goin' to happen to yuh won't worry nobody, Kelby,' Oakroyd observed menacingly, his guns still pointed. Then he added: 'As for me, I don't care how many guys I rub out: I've only one neck to stretch if they ever catch up on me . . .'

Still Parry said nothing, but the toe of his right half-boot edged a fraction forward so that it was just under the lip of a large, flat stone, of which there were dozens strewn about the canyon floor.

Motionless again he watched the outlaw as the merciless eyes contemplated him.

'The less marshals there is around

here the better for me, Kelby,' Oakroyd added. 'So — '

Parry acted — trusting everything to his aim. His right foot shot up and carried the flat stone with it. It whizzed diagonally and hit the outlaw clean in the face.

Not particularly hurt but definitely thrown off his guard, he fired both his guns simultaneously — far off the mark.

Then Parry closed with him, landed a short-armed jab to the side of the jaw that knocked him backwards to crash into the dust. Parry seized one of the guns and wrenched it from the strong fingers. The other one exploded aimlessly and for the third time the canyon echoed with the noise.

A knee in his stomach sent Parry rocking back on his heels, winded. The gun exploded as he flung himself flat — then, despite the pain he was experiencing, he hurled himself forward in a flying tackle, gripped Oakroyd round the knees and brought him down, his gun jerking out of his hand.

A smashing uppercut snapped back his head but he returned it with interest, delivering a pile-driver fist into Parry's face.

Parry reared up, dazed, and, seizing his chance, Oakroyd scrambled to his feet. His back to the precipice, Parry clenched his fists and waited, then at the identical moment Oakroyd sprang at him he brought his fist down with smashing power on the back of the man's neck and crashed him to his knees, half stunned. This gave him the mastery.

He dived for the outlaw's second gun and levelled it alongside its twin.

'All right, Oakroyd, on your feet!' he ordered.

Slowly Oakroyd obeyed. His necker-chief had fallen from his face in the struggle and revealed the lean, stubbly features — cruel, hard, shifty. Parry reached forward and patted the man's pockets to satisfy himself that there were no other hidden weapons, then he frowned as from the shirt pocket he pulled forth a wad of notes.

'Plenty of money for a skunk like you, isn't it?' he said drily. 'Some more of your thievin', eh?'

'That money was given to me!' Oakroyd snapped. 'There wasn't no thievin' about it . . . '

He was bitter, furious, at the thought that he had been captured. He knew perfectly well that a man as trained as Parry Kelby would not give him the faintest chance of turning the tables.

Now, being cornered, it was consistent with Jeff Oakroyd's shallow nature that he did not see any reason why he alone should be brought to trial. He gave a slow, vicious smile.

'If yuh think I'm the biggest game yuh can get, Kelby, you're loco,' he said briefly. 'There's a sheriff over in Dry Acres who's worth the pickin' up. *He* gave me that money — all twenty-five hundred of it, an' there was another twenty-five hundred to come if I rubbed out a certain person.'

Parry put the money in his hip-pocket. 'Keep talking,' he said.

'He give me the money an' the rest of it will be in the branch of a sycamore tree at the end o' the trail outside the town,' Oakroyd said sourly. 'Or I reckon it *would* have been there if I'd have taken care o' this guy who does a lot o' talkin' from a buckboard — Carson by name. Same swine as got Glanton killed!' he finished viciously.

Parry listened carefully. He knew of the part Blake Carson had played in Glanton's downfall, having read the report of Standish. Maybe he was about to learn some information that would be useful for his own investigation . . .

By degrees Oakroyd got out the details, making the implications for Binalt as black as he possibly could. He finished with his slow, cold smile.

'I reckon that guy Binalt might as well be picked up same as me, Kelby.'

'You would — being that particular type of sidewinder,' Parry answered. 'No sense of loyalty even towards those of your own kidney. Right now, though, we're taking a ride back to Caradoc. I'll attend to this sheriff of Dry Acres later. Go and get your horse.'

For answer Oakroyd whistled sharply and his pinto came loping forward from behind the rock spur. Parry waited for it to come up and then waved his gun.

'Get in your saddle, Oakroyd.'

The outlaw hesitated, furious at the realization that he had no guarantee whatever that Parry Kelby had believed his story about the sheriff of Dry Acres. The fact that he couldn't drag somebody else down with him in his defeat was too much for him.

He forgot the levelled guns, forgot everything, and hurled himself on Parry in tearing fury.

Parry did not fire because his man was unarmed. Instead he dropped one gun and lashed up his fist with devastating power into Oakroyd's stomach.

The outlaw doubled over, anguished, then a right hook took him in the jaw.

He jerked straight, stumbled backwards — outwards — and suddenly vanished over the canyon's lip. It had been much nearer than Parry had imagined.

Quickly recovering from the shock, Parry dived to the precipice and stared over its edge. He was in time to see the outlaw's falling body strike the out-jutting rocks with sickening impact — once, twice, and then plunge into the surging waters of the river below.

Parry only reflected for a split second. He had not got Jeff Oakroyd on his agenda, of course, but it was his duty as a marshal to bring him in, dead or alive. Even as he thought of this he dived outwards into space — down, down, for seemingly endless distance, hit the water, and plunged under.

As he sank down deeply Parry felt a shock to his body at the abrupt change in temperature. His impetus carried him almost to the bottom of the river. Twisting his body upright, he kicked his legs and rose to the surface. He let out his breath in a great gasp, and looked about him.

He caught sight of Oakroyd being swept away by the current, then hit out with vigorous overarm strokes, rapidly overtaking the outlaw's senseless body as the current carried him along.

Grasping him by the collar of his shirt he dragged him broadside to the current and at last to the rocky shingle at the edge of the river and base of the cliff.

It was only then that Parry realized he had dragged out a sodden corpse.

Jeff Oakroyd was dead, the back of his head completely crushed by the force with which he had hit the rocks in his fall.

Breathing hard, steam rising from his sodden clothes and hair, Parry kneeled beside the body. As he did so a plan was forming in his mind.

He was conscious now of the fact that he had a heaven-sent chance, perhaps, to work his way into the confidence of the dubious sheriff of Dry

Acres without exciting that gentleman's suspicions.

This had been the angle which had been worrying him: how to find out what sort of a hold the sheriff had on the community — and for why — without letting him be aware of the fact. But *how*?

Parry gave a grim smile. Nine o'clock that evening, Oakroyd had said. That was when the talkative Carson on the buckboard had to be shot down. Nine o'clock. That allowed just about enough time to get back to Caradoc with Oakroyd's dead body, make out a report, and then return to Dry Acres at the time prescribed, and disguise himself as Oakroyd.

Parry knew from his headquarters' circular that Oakroyd's usual method of operating was to remain masked, so it was unlikely that Oakroyd had revealed his features to Binalt on his first meeting. Anyway, it was a chance that Parry was prepared to take. In every other particular he resembled the outlaw — tall, rangy, pale-blue eyes, and with the man's own pinto, guns, clothes, and original twenty-five hundred dollars in his pocket —

Yes, Binalt would be fooled, never suspect there had been a switch in identities. He would have no reason to — as for killing Carson where he stood on the buckboard, well, that could be fixed somehow. Lastly, Oakroyd's uneducated drawl would be relatively easy to fake.

Parry nodded to himself and felt in his hip-pocket for money and wallet. The money and contents of the wallet were sodden with the river water, but intense sunlight would soon take care of that.

From the wallet he also took the official detailed note from headquarters that gave the description of Jeff Oakroyd. It was a much more thorough analysis than that contained in the various reward-dodgers stuck on trees and telegraph poles throughout the region, and carried the heading of the authorities in Caradoc City.

Parry read the details through and compared the facts with the dead man beside him. There was no mistake about it: it was Jeff Oakroyd all right — and anyway, the dead man had as good as admitted it.

Putting the money in his shirt pocket, where in time the sun's heat would dry it, he returned the wallet to his hip-pocket with the official detailed list inside it.

Then he rose and turned to survey the cliff for a way back to the canyon floor and the horses.

5

Evening was upon Dry Acres. The cobalt-blue of the western sky was feathered with vermilion and gold. The murdering heat of the day was shortly to give place to the biting cold of night as the stored-up warmth escaped irresistibly into the unclouded vacuum.

In the main streets of the ramshackle little town kerosene lamps gleamed from the stores, shacks, and bunkhouses, and particularly outside the Black Slipper. From the unlighted window of his office Henry Binalt watched and smiled. He was alone. Standing on a buckboard at his usual chosen time, as regular as a prophet presaging the end of the world, Blake Carson would soon be conducting another election speech. It was unlikely that the events of the morning would have shaken him much. By degrees a little knot of people would gather, and listen. And then . . .

In Binalt's inside coat pocket, securely sealed in an envelope, was $2,500, and his horse was waiting patiently beside the tie rail. The moment Jeff Oakroyd appeared *and* wiped out Carson — that was the essential thing! — Henry Binalt would satisfy himself as to Carson's death and then make a trip to the sycamore tree.

He was not going to attempt a double-cross because it would not pay him to do so.

Also surveying the evening on the trail just outside the town was Parry Kelby, dressed complete with black neckerchief face-mask as Jeff Oakroyd.

Same pinto, same guns, same figure — vastly different motives. Three miles behind him he had left his colleague from headquarters, Walt Standish, with whom he intended to make contact later.

The already cool night wind from

the mountains had freshened Parry after the hard day's riding. Motionless, he kept Oakroyd's pinto in the shadow of a giant cactus.

There was a full hour to go yet before nine o'clock, an hour in which Parry could study the town's layout and mentally check over his plan.

The main street was plain enough: there'd be no mistake about that, and not far away from him, ghostly now against the darkening sky, was the sycamore tree, where, providing he killed the young speech-maker on the buckboard, $2,500 would shortly be lying. If his plan worked as he intended there would be no killing and therefore no money, but there might be the chance of entering into Binalt's confidence . . .

The night deepened. The cold breath of the dark stirred from the mesa like a restless spirit and disturbed the pinto's mane in its passage. Parry Kelby sat motionless, masked, a lone watcher.

The yuccas, the cacti, the brittle-bush, the sage: they all foundered in a common haze and became featureless. There were rustlings in the baked earth as lizards and desert rats shifted their quarters; a faint whirring from a sidewinder which made the pinto raise his head uneasily . . .

Then the night, swift as a soundless giant, and the glow of the stars in the purple dome which had become the sky.

Still Parry waited — but now things were taking shape. From a side-turning amidst the wooden buildings of the high street a buckboard and team suddenly appeared and came to a stop beside the boardwalk, some fifty yards from the Black Slipper.

A figure, young and strong, with a Stetson on the back of his head, began to talk and wave his arms.

Parry could not hear what he was saying but he judged correctly that this was Blake Carson, the man he was supposed to kill.

Neck-reining the pinto, he spurred it gently forward until he was within earshot, watching the young man in the light of the flaring kerosene lamps. Already a small group of men and women had gathered, listening intently.

'So that's the issue,' Parry muttered to himself presently. 'An election speech — either Binalt or Carson for it. In other words, this one has to be fixed so's to give Binalt a clear run. But why in tarnation should a man *want* such a hold over such a place for? Looks hell-fried to me.'

He eased one of the outlaw's .38s from its holster, made sure his neckerchief was in position, and then prepared for action.

Still beside his office window, gazing out on the scene, Henry Binalt also watched. Disquieting fears that perhaps Oakroyd had decided to keep the $2,500 he had already got and forgo the remainder were upon him. He was just the kind of skunk who might do that . . .

Then came action — and Binalt sharpened to attention. The figure of a masked rider on a pinto came hurtling down the main street, his guns firing, chiefly in the air. One red flash aimed directly at Carson however, but the bullet must have missed him for he remained standing and watching the careering gunman as he went on up the main street.

Immediately Binalt dashed outside to the boardwalk and stared at where the lone horseman was vanishing into the distance of kerosene light. He looked across at the untouched Carson and his face darkened with fury.

There would be no journey to the sycamore tree with the remaining $2,500. Oakroyd had failed and Carson still remained to be eradicated. Sum total — $2,500 dead loss!

'I reckon it's about time we rustled a posse together and went and roped in that *hombre*,' observed a cowhand immediately below Binalt's office tie rail.

Binalt forced himself to be attentive to the faces now looking towards him.

'Yeah, that's right!' somebody else agreed. 'He already came a-shootin' through here this mornin' — an' we're just lettin' him. What about it, Sheriff?'

'He's too fast for us,' Binalt answered, trying to control his angry disappointment. 'And, anyway, we'd never find him in the dark. I'll let Caradoc City know he's been seen twice in this territory and let them start looking. They'll fix it quicker than we could.'

It was a lame excuse and he knew it, but he was in no mood to argue the point. Bitter at the outlaw's failure to work according to plan he returned into the office that displayed his nameplate prominently outside, lighted the oil-lamp and drew down the blind.

Scowling, he threw himself in the swivel-chair at the desk and reflected. A perfectly good scheme gone wrong for which he would have been more than willing to part with the remaining $2,500.

He remained brooding for perhaps ten minutes, trying to devise some alternative scheme, then he gave a start and turned as the office door opened — he remembered he had not locked it — and a tall masked figure came in silently, a .38 pointing from his right hand.

'Oakroyd!' Binalt gasped, staring. 'How in hell did you get in town again? You've got your gall!'

'Yeah, that's right,' Parry Kelby — 'Oakroyd' — agreed calmly. 'I got my gall. Yuh get that way when folks are on the prod for yuh. I doubled back into town and slipped in here when things was quiet. My cayuse is fastened round the side outa sight. I thought I owed yuh an explanation for tonight.'

'All right, but you don't have to level that rod at me, do you? I thought we were supposed to be friends.'

'I ain't got no friends,' Parry answered coldly, from behind the neckerchief-mask. 'Leastways, not now that Glanton's been wiped out.'

Binalt got to his feet and locked the office door. Then he looked at the keen, steady eyes over the neckerchief.

'Well, what happened?' he demanded bluntly. 'Your job was to get Carson — that man on the buckboard. Why didn't you hit him with that shot you fired?'

'My cayuse jolted me at the last second, I reckon,' Parry shrugged. 'Put me off my bead — an' at the speed I was goin' I only had time for the one shot.' The explanation was a reasonable one, but Binalt still scowled darkly.

'But,' Parry resumed, 'I reckon that if I stick around for a day or two I'll figure somethin' else. I means to earn that remainin' twenty-five hundred an' add it to this . . . ' He raised the now dried notes in his shirt pocket, chiefly to verify his bogus identity, and then slid them back in again.

'A day or two!' Binalt looked at him

fixedly. 'But you can't! Everybody'd know you.'

Parry holstered his gun and leaned his elbows casually on the top of the desk. 'Listen, Binalt, there ain't nobody here knows me by my face leastways. With this mask off an' another set o' clothes I'd simply be just another stranger in town. An' that's what I'm a-goin' to be while I figure out a new, quiet way to put this jigger Carson where we both want him — six feet under! Yuh never saw my face, did yuh?' Parry waited in real anxiety for the answer to his question. Upon it depended his whole scheme, whether he should stay or back out quickly. To his relief Binalt shook his head.

'Of course not, not with that mask you're still wearin'. But I don't like the idea. It's dangerous.'

'Yeah? From what I've seen on it it's even more dangerous — to you — for Carson to keep on shoutin' his face off. Election's back of it, huh?'

'Well, yes,' Binalt admitted, shrugging. 'I've got to be sure that I win re-election, that's all.'

'Why?'

Binalt tightened his lips and made no answer. With a shrug Parry took off the neckerchief and returned it to his throat. Then he cuffed up his black Stetson, aware that Binalt was studying him intently. Now had come the acid test.

'For an outlaw you're not as desperate looking as I'd expected,' Binalt commented finally. He reflected, feeling unsure whether the outlaw's eyes had been grey and not pale blue — unless it had been the poor light in the Black Slipper. Then he relaxed. Of course it was Jeff Oakroyd because it simply could not be anybody else. He had the money, the facts, everything.

'Yeah,' Parry said musingly, looking about him. 'I reckon I might do a good deal worse 'n settle in this town for a while. It's just the kinda place I been hankerin' after. Be a good chance to lie low for a while, an' in fresh clothes I'd be safe.' He gave Binalt an insolent glance, then went on:

'Yuh'd better get me some — an' in case you're thinkin' of arguin' just remember that if I get caught I can tell plenty. Twenty-five hundred dollars, which I ain't aimin' to spend until I get the rest of it, would sure take some explainin' from an *hombre* like me. I'll tell 'em where I *got* it . . . Savvy? So you an' me had better understand each other, huh?'

Binalt considered for a moment or two and then gave a slow nod.

'All right, if that's how you want it. I want Carson out of the way before the election, which is in a few days, so I'll help you get settled.'

'OK. In that case I'm a-goin' to be a friend of yourn who's just blown into town, see? Nobody, not even a marshal, I reckon, would ever expect an outlaw to be a friend o' the mayor and sheriff, 'specially when this mornin' yuh went a-gunnin' for me in the saloon. The tie-up's sweet an' natural, like. An' me name'll be Joe Calvert from now on.'

'What about your horse? It's quite a distinctive pinto and could be recognized.'

'Not the way I aim to fix it. Once I've gotten that change o' clothes from yuh I'll ride that cayuse into the desert and leave it there. Lack o' water an' too much sun'll do the rest. Yuh'll loan me a horse while I'm in town, an' I'll have enough money to buy another afore I leave — grantin' I don't frisk one. I got it all doped out, Binalt. All I'll need then is a suitcase to put these clothes in — 'sides makin' it look as though I'm a visitor.'

Though he did not show it Binalt found the man's cold grin discomforting. 'And where are you goin' to bunk?' he asked. 'Certainly not with me: I'm not standing having an outlaw as a ranch guest. An' I don't want you in the Black Slipper, either.'

Parry only grinned the wider. 'OK, I'm not exactly a-hankerin' after bein' tied to your gunstraps myself. I'll bunk at the best roomin'-house in this cockeyed town.'

'You'd better go to Ma Falkner's. Plenty of room there.'

'Right — an' yuh can pay for it. You're the mayor and yuh can't do without me. Call it expenses.'

Binalt's mouth was ugly. 'All right,' he agreed sourly.

'Now you'd better wait here, without the light, while I go back to my spread for an outfit for you. It'll be a bit big for you but maybe you'll manage.'

'I reckon I will,' Parry agreed and cupping his hand round the chimney-glass of the lamp, he blew out the flame.

★ ★ ★

It was towards eleven o'clock when the horseman came galloping out of the night. Marshal Walt Standish, comfortable beside his camp-fire, looked up expectantly and his hand strayed to his gun, then he got up with a smile of welcome as the gleaming sides of a pinto came into the range of the firelight and Parry Kelby swung down from the saddle.

He was attired in a check shirt, riding-pants somewhat too large, half-boots, and a white Stetson. A red neckerchief completed the outfit.

'OK, Walt, take this pinto back to Caradoc and don't let it stray back here,' he said briefly. 'I've gotten myself in with Binalt, even though I don't know yet what his game is.'

'Binalt himself, eh?' Standish was interested. 'Then you've found that my suspicions about him were justified?'

'Pretty well, from what little I've learned. He's sold on the idea that I'm Oakroyd — hence these clothes he's loaned me. Only thing I'm wearing now which belonged to Oakroyd are his thirty-eights.' He slapped the crossover holsters.

'What happens now, then?' Standish asked.

'No idea as yet: I shall simply act as circumstances dictate. One thing I have discovered is that Binalt is plumb scared of losing the coming election. Why he wants to keep his grip on a cockeyed dump like Dry Acres is something I've yet to find out. If there should be anything of vital importance, Walt, I'll find a way to get in touch — but not by telegraph: that might be dangerous . . . '

'And what if I need to contact *you*?'

Parry reflected. 'If you need to contact me — but only in case of life or death — I'll be staying at Ma Falkner's, known as Joe Calvert. Now I've got to be getting back. Binalt's waiting to take me to Ma Falkner's as his guest. He thinks I'm turning this horseflesh loose in the desert.'

The two men shook hands and then parted, Parry walking back as far as the trail and then carrying on towards Dry Acres, which he reached once more an hour later. He found Binalt still waiting in his office.

'OK,' Parry said briefly. 'That cayuse won't bother us no more. From now on I'm a stranger in town. Let's get goin' to Ma Falkner's. We'll talk again in the mornin' an' I can figure out a new plan for takin' care o' Carson.'

Parry picked up the suitcase in which he had packed the outlaw's clothes and with a nod Binalt got to his feet. He still looked as though he didn't like the way things were shaping.

6

Ma Falkner, rotund, slatternly, was not the type of woman to inspire confidence in any guest, but at least she had the saving grace of being extremely easy-going and for this reason accepted all Binalt's explanations concerning the uneducated stranger — whom he introduced as 'Joe Calvert' — without comment.

She did not even complain at being raked out of bed after midnight to accept her new boarder. With a dressing-gown hugged about her obese figure and an oil-lamp in her hand she showed Parry his room, small, but good enough for his purposes, and then left him to his own devices after she had collected a week's rent in advance from Binalt.

Parry slept well, entirely content with his actions up to date, and came down to breakfast in the large front dining-room to find himself introduced to the other boarders. Ma Falkner, still untidy, was at the head of the table, and a thin-faced girl in a cotton frock and crooked apron was doing all the serving.

Beyond nodding and muttering a few words Parry did not pay any attention to the other boarders. He delayed over his breakfast until he and Ma Falkner, who was tucking into her second portion of bacon and eggs, were alone. Then he began to open up a little.

'I reckon I don't know much about this town, Ma. Anythin' yuh c'n tell me?'

The woman's fat-encircled eyes gazed at him. 'Tell you? What, f'rinstance?'

'Well — what sort of a place is it to be in? Expensive? Cheap? Big taxes? I'm sorta prospectin' for a place to settle.'

'The taxes around these parts'll cripple you,' the woman answered, with a sullen droop to her mouth. 'You say you're a friend o' Sheriff Binalt's?'

As Parry nodded she went on sourly, 'Then you're no friend o' mine, even if you is a boarder here. Binalt's taxes is cripplin' all of us bit by bit — but since we put him in power we've only ourselves to thank.'

'Has Binalt given any kind o' explanation for the taxes?' Parry asked thoughtfully.

'He *says* the money is bein' put aside for land development, but we ain't seen anythin' like that happenin' yet — an' between you an' me I'm wonderin' if we ever shall.'

'How come you're still here then, Ma?' Parry asked, fishing for more information.

'Me? I can keep goin' because I don't do so badly with this place o' mine — not much competition 'cept for the Black Slipper. But some of the homesteaders just have to sell out an' hit the trail. They just can't keep a-goin'.'

'Then why d'yuh stand for it?' Parry

demanded, trying to win back the woman's confidence. 'If yuh know your rights, why don't yuh do somethin' about it? There's plenty o' men in town, what I've seen on 'em. Binalt may be an acquaintance o' mine, but if he's double-crossin' all o' yuh I'd be the first to admit he deserves all he gets.'

'Ain't that easy,' the woman said morosely. 'He's got about a dozen gunhawks that tail around with him — one in particular by name of Brad Dugan.' She shrugged helplessly. 'Takin' care of Binalt would take care o' us, too, I reckon. Only hope we've got is gettin' him out at the comin' election. Young Blake Carson — he's straight as a gun barrel — would make a lot o' difference to the old place.'

'Yeah . . . ' Parry reflected for a moment and decided against saying anything more. He had found out all he wanted.

That Binalt had some mysterious reason of his own for the imposition of crushing taxes had been obvious for some time; now it was also clear that he had the populace inexorably under his thumb.

The problem now was to find the motive behind it all.

Parry left the rooming-house in a thoughtful mood and lounged across the dusty street to Binalt's office.

As he had anticipated, the men and women crowding the street took no notice of him; and certainly they didn't connect him with the affrays the previous morning and night.

He smiled to himself as upon one of the two-by-four posts at the end of the boardwalk he beheld a reward dodger: the picture of a masked gunman in a black Stetson, underneath which was the caption:

$10,000! DEAD OR ALIVE!
THE ABOVE SUM WILL BE PAID TO
ANYBODY GIVING INFORMATION
CONCERNING JEFFREY OAKROYD,
WANTED FOR MURDER.
ALL REPORTS TREATED AS

CONFIDENTIAL.
HENRY BINALT, ARTHUR KAYNE, DRY ACRES, CARADOC CITY.

Parry found Binalt in his office, at the roll-top desk, the lanky cold-eyed Brad Dugan standing beside him. Their eyes went suspiciously over Parry as he entered.

'Howdy,' Parry greeted, and as he glanced up from his desk Binalt gave a grunt of acknowledgment. Then with a jerk of his head he sent Dugan slouching out of the office.

'Well, what's on your mind?' Binalt took his cheroot from his mouth and turned in his chair, surveying Parry as he half-lounged with his elbows on top of the desk. 'Any plans yet for dealing with Carson? I want to be gettin' things movin'. The sooner Carson is taken care of and you're out of town the better I'll like it.'

'I ain't in no hurry,' Parry answered, shrugging. 'In fact, I kinda like it here — an' it sure is safe when you're the friend o' the mayor an' sheriff. How about that cayuse yuh was goin' to get for me?'

'I've got a sorrel you can borrow,' Binalt said. 'You'll find it tied to the hitch rail outside, next to a brown bay, which is mine. But you've more things to do than to ride around admirin' the scenery, Oakroyd — '

'Calvert's the name!' Parry snapped. 'An' don't yuh go forgettin' it, neither.'

'Calvert then. As I said, your job is to fix Carson, not spend your time roaming about on a borrowed horse.'

'I'll fix Carson when I'm good an' ready. In the meantime don't forget I've twenty-five hundred dollars on me that can still make for plenty of awkward questions for you. I . . . '

Parry broke off and glanced towards the door as it opened abruptly and a girl came in. He noted interestedly that she was blonde-headed, small-featured, with a practical and rather pretty face. Her height was around five feet four and she was dressed in a silk checker-board shirt, grey riding-pants, and half-boots.

'Here it is, chiseller,' she said curtly, and flung down a long sealed envelope on the desk blotter. Then she stood looking at Binalt and fingering the scarlet neckerchief at her throat.

Binalt hesitated, apparently some-what embarrassed. He jerked his head for Parry to leave but he affected not to notice. Instead Parry divided his attention between the envelope and the slender girl beside him.

Binalt cleared his throat. 'After all, Miss Dalman, there isn't any call for you to take it this way . . . '

'I think, there is!' Her voice was cold. 'What it amounts to is that you've swindled my father and me out of our property, same as you have with a lot of other homesteaders around here. What you want is jail, Mr Binalt, and I'm not so sure but what you won't get it in the finish. Blake Carson isn't such a fool, you know.'

Binalt set his mouth and hooked a thumb in the envelope flap. He peered inside at what seemed to be a legal deed, scrutinized a signature, and then nodded.

'All right, that's OK,' he said, meeting the girl's blue eyes. 'Be out in six days. I'll take over then.'

Without another word, though her expression was infinitely disgusted, the girl left the office and slammed the door.

Binalt got up and took the envelope and its contents over to the safe. Parry, hands in his pants' pockets, lounged over to the window and watched the girl untying the reins of a small mare from the hitch rail outside.

As Parry watched, she swung into the saddle — at least, this was what she intended doing, but the saddle, evidently insecurely buckled, abruptly slipped sideways.

The sudden, unexpected movement startled the sensitive animal.

The horse lunged, reared her forelegs

in the air, gave a whinny — and then began running, the girl half in the saddle and half out of it, struggling frantically to raise herself out of line of the flying hoofs.

'I'll be back . . . ' Parry flung the brief words at Binalt, who still hovered by the safe, then in one concerted rush he was out of the office and on to the back of the sorrel Binalt had brought for his use.

To unhitch the reins was but the work of a second, then in a cloud of dust he was hurtling after the runaway as it careered madly at the far end of the main street, watched by wondering men and women, upon none of whom it seemed to dawn that the girl was likely to be killed if she was not helped quickly.

Parry had realized it, however, and spurred the sorrel to all the speed he could make, which was considerable. The hoofs tearing up the dust, hot wind blowing in his face, Parry crouched low on the beast's mane and encouraged it to go faster and faster — out of the town and along the dusty, sun-drenched trail which led out to the mesa and, eventually, Caradoc City.

As the animals raced on, Parry gradually narrowed the distance between them. First it was a distance of several hundred yards, then it decreased to a couple of dozen — then feet, and at last Parry drew level. Leaning out of his saddle he caught the half-balanced girl round the waist and held her tightly.

'Shake your feet out of the stirrups,' he panted. 'Quick! I've got you safely . . . ' She wasted no time arguing and Parry realized that in the excitement he had let slip the uncouth voice of 'Oakroyd'.

Frantically the girl kicked her feet free and the saddle slipped round again until it was underneath the animal's belly — in which position the girl would undoubtedly have been killed but for Parry's intervention.

With a final lunge she dragged herself

free. Parry lowered her gently until her feet touched the ground and she began running. Then he released her and charged after the maddened mare.

In a few minutes he caught up, seized the reins, tugged, coaxed, forced up the head, began bringing the animal back, snorting, the whites of her eyes showing in crescents of fright.

Seconds later the girl caught up with him. She was breathing hard, with her hair dishevelled, and was chafing her hands where she had clung on desperately. But otherwise she appeared unharmed.

She stood waiting as Parry got off his horse and stooped to examine the mare's saddle.

He unbuckled it, put it back into the normal position and made sure it was tight. Then he looked up to meet the girl's blue eyes. He remembered his false identity just in time and hoped she had not noticed the tone of his voice in those other desperate moments.

'I reckon yuh should be OK now, miss,' he said.

'You — saved my life,' she answered, hesitating. 'I don't know what to say, to show you how truly grateful I am.' She smiled ruefully, and nodded at her horse. 'It was my own fault. I saddled her myself, but I was in such a foul temper before setting out to see the mayor I guess I did it badly . . . ' A little frown clouded her forehead, and she hesitated again. Then:

'I don't seem to remember ever seeing you around this district. Who are you?'

'The name's Joe Calvert. I only got into town last night. I'm a friend o' mayor Binalt's.'

'Oh, you are!' Ann Dalman's look of puzzlement changed to one of acute disappointment; her lips tightened. 'That's a pity. Anybody who's a friend of Binalt is no friend of mine, even though I do appreciate what you did for me.'

The girl came forward and took the

reins of the now passive mare. 'I'd better be on my way,' she said quietly.

Parry did not answer. He was watching his sorrel as its forefeet kneaded restlessly at the dry, dusty earth. But it was not all sun-baked soil he raked up. There was something else — yellowish, powdery, with a faint glitter.

'Don't go, miss,' Parry said abruptly, and the girl took her hand from the saddle horn and regarded him coolly.

'Why not? I've nothing to stop for.'

'I think mebby yuh have, miss. Yuh must be plenty shaken after what yuh just went through. Here — sit down and rest awhile.'

Parry motioned to the shade of a towering rock spur. The girl only hesitated for a moment, then she walked over to him and they settled in the shadow. Puzzled, the girl looked at Parry's lean brown face and blue eyes.

'As yuh know, miss, I was in Binalt's office this mornin' when yuh came in . . . '

'Yes, I know. I saw you.'

'What was it all about? What's he done to chisel yuh?'

'Oh — that.' She gave a tired little smile. 'Now I *know* you're a stranger in town otherwise you'd know all about it. To put it briefly, Binalt imposes such heavy taxes on the homesteaders here that they just can't be paid, in the majority of cases, anyway. The concession Binalt makes in that case is that he'll take over their property by deed-transfer in return for the unpaid taxes.' There was acid bitterness in the girl's voice.

'That's what's happened to my father and me. We've been struggling to raise money for some time, especially after our ranch burned down and had to be rebuilt. Last month I inherited some property in town — my late uncle's newspaper press and offices.' She hesitated, obviously finding her recollections painful.

'I'd planned on re-opening the paper myself, later on — after I'd helped Dad get things straight at the ranch. But . . . ' the girl gave a shrug. 'We've found the going too tough so now we've transferred the offices to Binalt, and we've six days in which to vacate — '

'Then that was the transfer deed I saw yuh hand to him?'

'Yes. The actual negotiations began some time ago. But that's only paid off our existing debts. We've exhausted all our resources to keep up with the taxes and the next step will be that we'll have to continue selling our cattle, and that will put our ranch itself at risk. Some of the other local ranchers — who didn't have other properties in town — have already transferred their land to Binalt . . . '

She smiled faintly at Parry, who had been listening closely.

'I don't really know why I'm telling you this, Mr Calvert. I'm Ann Dalman, by the way. My father and I have the Roaring G just outside Dry Acres.'

'I'm glad you did, Miss Dalman. I may be able to help you,' Parry said.

Then as the girl glanced at him wonderingly, he added:

'An' what does Binalt *do* with these ranches and homesteads when he's bought 'em?'

'Nothing . . . ' Ann Dalman brushed a wisp of blonde hair out of her eyes and gazed absently towards the grey mountains. 'Nothing at all! That's what I don't understand! He's no objection to us selling off our stock to try and pay taxes: all he does is take the land and property in lieu of them if we can't pay up. I suppose he has some sort of plan. But it's a rotten and corrupt way of doing things!' she burst out angrily, clenching her fists.

'It's . . . extortion! We're simply being *made* to sell out to him whether we like it or not!'

'Yeah . . . that's exactly what it is.' Parry meditated, his mind working swiftly, then he looked about him and asked a surprising question.

'Have yuh lived long around these parts, Miss Dalman?'

The girl looked puzzled. 'I was born here on the Roaring G spread. Why?'

'I was just a-wonderin' if yuh could tell me somethin' since I'm new around these parts. This trail here, goin' between these mountains — I reckon it was once part of a river, huh? That the trail itself is now a big arroyo?'

'Possibly,' the girl admitted. 'In fact, probably. This town hasn't always been called Dry Acres. I seem to remember reading somewhere that a river went through here, then a landslide blocked and diverted it.'

'Which makes all the land around here part of a dried-up watercourse! That's interestin', mebby . . . ' then before the girl could question his speculations Parry added: 'If yuh have to sell out eventually, what do you reckon on doin'?'

'That depends. Father has another relative in Arrow Point that's about fifty miles from here. If things got desperate we could move there. But that won't happen if Binalt loses the forthcoming election.'

'Yuh mean the new man might repeal the taxes?'

The girl laughed. 'No *might* about it, Mr Calvert. He *will*! Blake Carson is my fiancé!'

'Carson!' Parry gave a start. 'Yuh mean he . . . That is, *you* . . . Y'mean the jigger who's doin' all the talkin' in the street?'

'That's right.' Ann Dalman smiled. 'He's putting up for election in an effort to get Binalt out of office. We've only just become engaged, and I guess our future depends on whether he wins the election. He isn't entirely confident. Binalt's doing all he can — including using shooting-irons — to stop him.'

Parry was silent, trying to figure something out of the new, unexpected twist in events. Then the girl got to her feet and looked down at him.

'I have to be going.' she said. 'I'm rested now — and thanks for all you did.' Parry scrambled up as she walked away gracefully to where her mare was standing. Reaching it, she stooped and looked at the saddle buckling anxiously — then apparently something else caught her eye in the dust. She stood looking at it. Finally she bent down and picked up a glittering object.

'Would this be . . . yours?' she asked, turning a surprised face.

Parry walked over to her and looked at the object in her outstretched palm. It was his marshal's badge. Even as he stared at it his hand strayed unconsciously to his left shirt-pocket.

The button had been wrenched off during his activities with the runaway mare, and the badge, which he had kept in that pocket in case of sudden need to prove his real identity, had evidently slipped out when he had stooped to buckle the saddle.

He met the girl's eyes. She had been watching his hand feeling the shirt pocket and placed her own conclusions upon the action.

'Yes,' Parry said quietly, relapsing

into his normal voice and taking the badge from her, 'it's mine. I'd rather have kept it secret, but things being as they are I reckon I'll have to throw myself on your mercy.'

She shook her head. 'Hardly a question of that. You saved my life, and I'll be only too glad of a chance to repay the debt — that is, if you want to say anything?'

Parry made up his mind on the spot, satisfied that the girl was worthy of trust. He'd read the files of his predecessor and knew the sterling part the girl had played with Blake Carson, in the case of Mark Glanton. He motioned back to where they had been seated and again they settled down.

'I'm Parry Kelby,' he explained, 'from Caradoc City headquarters. My precise reason for being in this district is to investigate the activities of Binalt. Over a month ago, as you know, one of my colleagues came to this town — '

'Of course!' Ann exclaimed, her eyes bright. 'It was Blake who called him in!'

She frowned. 'Now what was his name? Stanhope? No ... Standish! That was it!'

'Marshal Walt Standish,' Parry smiled. 'And you must be the girl who helped him. I've seen the files ... '

'But Standish came here to investigate Mark Grayson — or rather, Glanton, the outlaw,' Ann frowned. 'But I thought all that had been sorted out? There wasn't anything linking Grayson to Binalt, was there?'

'Not directly,' Parry admitted. 'But Standish had his suspicions. Headquarters reckoned they couldn't send the same marshal back again without putting Binalt on his guard and maybe destroying evidence — so I was handed the assignment. Last night I came into town in the guise of Jeff Oakroyd, the outlaw, and — '

'You did! But — but how ... ?'

Parry swiftly outlined the circumstances and from his pocket pulled the official information sheet concerning Oakroyd. The girl read it through and then nodded slowly.

'Since you are such an intimate friend of young Carson I think you can be of great help in bringing Binalt to book,' Parry went on slowly.

'I'm willing,' the girl said firmly.

'Good girl! I've got a scheme at the back of my mind, but to work it out in detail I'll have to have a talk with Carson himself — and I don't mean at his store in Dry Acres, either. Somewhere quiet, less conspicuous. Do you think you could arrange it?'

'Yes, I think so,' the girl assented, reflecting. 'You can meet him at the Roaring G. Tonight if you like.'

'That'll do fine. Make it tonight at ten. It'll be dark then and nobody'll see me riding out of town. What's the quickest trail to get to the spread from Dry Acres?'

The girl gave him explicit directions and then added, 'The only thing is — I may find it hard to convince Blake of the facts. About you being a marshal, I mean ... especially after

129

he was shot at by Oakroyd!'

'Then keep that notice about him,' Parry told her. 'Only operatives from headquarters have those. That should convince him quick enough when you tell him where you got it.'

The girl nodded and put it in her shirt pocket.

'I think,' Parry finished, 'I've guessed the reason for Binalt's taxes and buying-up racket. What he's trying to get is all the land around these parts cheap. And I don't blame him. Come and take a look here . . . '

Ann rose and followed him to where his sorrel was standing. He had stopped scraping the earth now. Parry stooped and lifted a handful of dirt into his palm. As he stirred it with his fingers there were bright yellow glints.

'Just a lucky chance on my part that I happened to notice it,' he commented. 'It's gold-dust, I reckon. I'd never have happened on it but for this horse of mine digging it up. My guess is that there was a watercourse through here at one time, with a good deal of gold-bearing rock in the current. It got ground down, as rocks will, and when the river dried up the gold-dust remained under the surface. And if there is gold-*dust* there's likely to be a lot of real gold some place — but exactly *where* probably only Binalt knows. I'll wager that's his reason — '

'It must be!' the girl broke in excitedly. 'This land around here, and the other land he's trying to get, could become worth a fabulous fortune to him. The whole plot is becoming clear! And it explains why he's just got to be re-elected mayor and levy taxes and buy up the property and land of defaulters.'

'So I believe. But there's one important thing,' Parry cautioned her. 'Not a word of this to anybody, not even to your fiancé, Blake Carson. Any hint of gold would start an army of prospectors on the move and every plan to defeat Binalt would be blown sky-high. As things are we want to get him behind bars and then return the various properties to the rightful owners and — since he isn't a fully constituted sheriff and mayor — declare his actions illegal. The rightful owners will then be entitled to claim the particular value of the land which is theirs.'

Ann was nodding her head rapidly as Parry talked. 'Yes — yes, I understand. All this means that instead of just being a ramshackle town on the edge of nowhere, Dry Acres may finally become a really wealthy and important city!'

'More unlikely things have happened, Miss Dalman,' Parry agreed. 'A fact of which Henry Binalt is well aware . . . ' He paused to help the girl into the saddle of her mare.

'So,' he finished, 'not a word to anybody until I say so. And I'll be at your ranch at ten.'

7

During his ride back to Dry Acres Parry had plenty of time to think out the details of the plan he had devised.

It was one that certainly entailed a large element of risk, to say nothing of playing his wits against those of Henry Binalt, but these were both factors to which he looked forward. So by the time he had returned to Binalt's office in the main street and resumed the set expression he considered correct for Oakroyd, he knew exactly what he intended to do.

Binalt was at his desk as usual and looked up with a grim scowl as Parry came into his office.

'Where in blue hell did you go?' he demanded. 'You've been away over an hour! I thought you'd skipped town.'

'Not while I've twenty-five hundred to collect,' Parry assured him, taking off

133

his Stetson and throwing it down. 'I beat it like that because I'd seen that gal who came here was purty likely to be kicked to death by her cayuse if I didn't do somethin' pronto . . . the saddle had slipped.'

Parry would much rather not have given this explanation, but knowing a good percentage of the populace had watched his activities as he had raced down the main street he thought it safer. It made Binalt raise his heavy eyebrows.

'Oh?' He sat back in his swivel-chair. 'Since when did an ornery cuss like you take to savin' lives instead of blottin' 'em out? You're stepping right out of character, Oak — Calvert.'

Parry lighted a cigarette and watched Binalt over the match-flame whilst he thought out the next move. Then he said:

'I didn't go after that dame for the sheer sake o' savin' her, Binalt: I did it so's she'd be kinda grateful to me — which she were — an' perhaps tell

134

me as a reward why she handed over a transfer deed on property to yuh this mornin'.'

'Why, you damned snooper!' Binalt shouted, leaping up in fury. 'What's it got to do with you?'

'Plenty, I reckon,' Parry answered, unmoved. 'I'm a-thinkin' that that twenty-five hundred is pretty small dice when there's stuff so much bigger lyin' around here somewheres. That dame thinks there's gold in the land around here — an' I've sorta got to believin' her.'

'Gold!' Binalt's expression changed; then he began blustering. 'It's ridiculous! Gold — in a hole like Dry Acres? Hell, no!'

'Why not?' Parry demanded. 'Dry Acres is in Arizony, ain't it — an' there's lost gold-mines all over Arizony. Anybody will tell yuh that. And, 'sides, I've seen some o' the dust for myself. I ain't like the rest o' folks around here — I goes about with my eyes skinned because in my line I *have* to.'

135

Binalt sat down and lighted a cheroot. He had suddenly become icily calm. 'You're crazy,' he said curtly. 'An' so's that girl. If there was gold around here she wouldn't be keepin' it to herself. She'd be tellin' everybody and there'd be a rush and a hell of a lot of trouble from claim-jumpers.'

'She ain't *sure* — an' that's why she ain't said nothin' out loud. An' she won't be sayin' nothin' neither — she doesn't want to start a stampede in the town until she *is* sure. She only told me out o' gratitude for savin' her life.' Parry paused, waiting to see the effect of his words on Binalt. The last thing he wanted was to put the girl under risk of possible attack from Binalt.

Binalt's eyes glittered but he didn't say anything. Apparently he had accepted what had been said about the information remaining restricted.

'But,' Parry went on, 'I *am* sure, because to my way o' thinkin' there ain't no other reason why yuh'd be a-wantin' to tax the folks around here so fierce they have to transfer to yuh to pay their way. Yuh get the land an' property on the cheap — an' later yuh figure yuh'll cash in on a bonanza. You're not a-foolin' me, Binalt, even if you're a-foolin' yourself.'

'Are you trying to tell me I'm taking over the land just so's it'll be worth a fortune later?'

'I'm a-tellin' yuh — not *tryin'* to. An' I'll tell yuh what I'm a-goin' to do about it — You're a-goin' to give me fifty per cent on all tax profits yuh've made up to date — an' fifty per cent on everythin' yuh make in money from now on.'

'You're plain loco, Oakroyd! Besides, there ain't any gold. It's just a crazy story . . . ' Binalt stopped, looking into the muzzle of Parry's .38. The eyes above it were narrowed, hard as agate.

'I've nothin' to lose personally by rubbin' yuh out, Binalt — since I've rubbed out others afore yuh. The only thing I would lose is the position of the gold in this land — but if I *don't* get cut in for half of it yuh'll get nothin' at all. Only lead in your belly!' He glared threateningly at Binalt.

'There *is* gold around here, ain't there? It's back of your whole scheme, ain't it?'

Binalt was not fool enough to argue with a loaded .38 in the hand of an outlaw. He nodded his dark head helplessly.

'Yes, there is, and you're nothin' but a no-account blackmailer. And something else! Unless you take care of Carson there'll be nothin' *to* share. He'll see that neither of us gets anything. I've a lot more land and ranches to get yet — by forced measures — before I can start to open things in a big way.'

'Takin' care o' Carson,' Parry said, holstering his gun again, 'is part o' the job I'll do in return for my cut.'

'Big of you!' Binalt observed sourly. 'I should have got Brad Dugan to do the job and risked the publicity. Serves me right.'

'Mebby — but yuh didn't, an' now I knows all about your game it's too late to turn your back. I've still got my twenty-five hundred for evidence, don't forget — an' one wrong move out of yuh an' I'll make yuh smart. In plain lingo, Binalt, if the law gets me it gets you too — so start a-gettin' wise to yourself.'

Binalt bit hard on his cheroot. 'This means that you intend to stick around Dry Acres, then?'

'With a fortune in it what do you think? Yuh got yourself a partner, Binalt — an' just so's there no chance o' yuh gypping me I want to see the records of your taxes. Afore I took to the trail with a murder rap hangin' over me I used to be a purty good businessman. It seems to me that not all o' the homesteaders would be so hard pressed as that gal an' her pop was — needin' to transfer their property to pay up the taxes. So, afore I deal with Carson — an' I said a *afore* — I want to see just what yuh've made out of the taxes. Half o' whatever there is since yuh took office as sheriff is a-goin' to be mine. Savvy?'

Binalt hesitated. This was plain blackmail, as well as the naked exposure of his private racket. The records of the taxes he had collected were enough to condemn him in the eyes of the authorities, of which fact Parry himself was, of course, aware.

What Parry wanted, and, indeed, had got to have, was evidence — otherwise he could never arrest Binalt. It all depended now on whether Binalt considered the situation dangerous enough to fall into the trap.

In the few seconds while the two men measured each other quite a lot of thoughts went through Binalt's brain. With a lightning move he could probably shoot this parasite, remove the $2,500 he had with him, and turn him over to the law as Jeff Oakroyd and so collect the reward. $10,000 was not much, a mere drop in the ocean compared to the wealth which Binalt knew existed in Dry Acres' territory, but if he shot the outlaw what then?

Who would take care of Carson? Nobody known locally would do, and not for a moment did Binalt trust any of his own gunhawks sufficiently to be sure they would keep their mouths shut.

One would tell another, and if a dozen of them preyed on him as this one was preying now he would get nothing out of the deal at all. So perhaps one parasite — for whom a warrant for murder had been issued — was better than twelve who had no such fears.

Parry, too, was thinking things as the impasse persisted. As a marshal he could drop his pretence forthwith and charge Binalt with extortion and mishandling of public funds, thereafter taking him off to Caradoc City — granting the various gunhawks who guarded Binalt from places unseen would let him get away with it.

Further, arresting Binalt would not clean up the iniquity which flourished

141

in Dry Acres: it would require quite a few men from headquarters to clean up the 'little Binalts' afterwards.

Again, to charge Binalt and arrest him demanded proof, and to get the proof in the legal way, instead of by intimidation, he needed a search-warrant. While the warrant was obtained the evidence could easily be destroyed.

So, as Parry reasoned it, there was no other course but the one he was taking. Make Binalt give the evidence with his own hands. After that he could — and would — move fast enough.

'How much longer are yuh goin' to be?' Parry snapped abruptly. Binalt compressed his lips, got up, and went over to the safe.

From the safe he took a heavy ledger and planted it on top of the desk. Parry opened it and studied the items, jotting them down on a slip of paper.

His inward amazement at the gall of the man found no expression on his face. Finally, when he came to summing up the totals, he said slowly,

'Accordin' to my reckonin', Binalt — an' I'm believin' these items is plumb accurate since yuh made 'em for your own guidance — yuh've salted away about eighty thousand dollars so far — all out o' graft and corruption. I reckon I must be a sucker not to have dug myself up a nice little township an' racket just as good somewheres where there's gold ... OK, that's forty thousand dollars yuh owes me afore I makes a move.'

'Until you wipe out Carson you don't get a cent!' Binalt retorted.

Parry reflected and closed the ledger slowly. It was the answer he had been expecting.

'OK.' He shrugged. 'In the meantime I'll keep the book as security. I reckon yuh wouldn't like it to get into the wrong hands.'

Binalt's face hardened but he managed to control his temper — just.

'If that's the way you want it,' he

said, and Parry wondered what else was at the back of the man's mind that made him bow, apparently calmly, to the inevitable.

'What about Carson?' Binalt asked. 'What plans have you got to get him?'

'That's my business, ain't it? So long as I do get him what are yuh worryin' about?'

'Just this: I want to see you do it! I don't sort of feel inclined to take your word for it. What's your plan?'

'Well, I've got a nice simple one — with no fancy tricks like a-ridin' into town with a mask on. I'm a-goin' to shoot Carson when he's in the office of his timber store tomorrow night.'

'How'd you know he will be?' Binalt asked suspiciously.

'Because that dame Ann Dalman told me so! Didn't yuh know that she's a-figurin' to marry Carson?'

'She is?' Binalt looked astonished for a moment. 'No. First time I heard of it.'

'Now yuh know — an' the setup's a natural. I don't have to tell yuh that

that dame didn't know who I am — she simply figures I'm a stranger in town who saved her life. I got to know from her that Carson won't be givin' no more of his election speeches — too dangerous he reckons, which shows he's a yeller-belly anyway. That rules him out as a pot-shot for me when ridin' down the street, so, figurin' out a way to get at him I told the dame I was needin' some timber, on account o' my fixin' up a shack to live in in the town. I said I'd only have time to discuss business in an evenin' late on, when it's dark . . . '

'But if the dame knows you're goin' to see Carson, you'll be the chief suspect!' Binalt snapped.

Parry silenced him with a gesture.

'I've thought of that: hear me out. Finally I fixed it so's she'll tell Carson tonight when she sees him mebby — to stay in his office late tomorrow night to see me. OK, I goes an' sees him — but as Oakroyd, in a mask just in case I happen to be spotted — finish him off,

145

an' then use the darkness as a cover-up while I carry his body out to the mesa and leave it there. I'll dig the bullet out afore I leaves him so's there'll be no proof when — or if — he's found. The dame knows I'll be supposed to be seein' him, I reckon, an' she may think things. But even if she tries to pin the thing on me, without proof an' with no witnesses as to what I said, she can't do nothin'.'

'Mmm . . . that seems all right.' Binalt stroked his heavy jaw as he thought it out 'Only I reckon you won't mind me sayin' I don't trust you. I want to be sure that Carson is properly *dead* before I pay up. Just your word for it won't do for me. You might *think* you've killed him, then one day the body will get up and come walkin' into town!'

Parry had foreseen this, and was ready for it.

'Yuh can't come with me into his office: that'd look too durned suspicious, and he might get us in self-defence instead of us gettin' him. Since yuh don't trust me,' — a cold sneer curved Parry's lips — 'there ain't nothin' a-stoppin' yuh lookin' on through the window when I go in to him. But once I gets him out o' the office don't delay me. I'll have to get out to the mesa pronto.'

'All right,' Binalt agreed slowly. 'I reckon I'll have to make do with somethin' like that. But I'll make time to look at him when you bring him out of the office. In the meantime take good care of that ledger.'

Parry nodded and hunched it up under his arm. 'I will. It's my security against the money yuh owe me — and yuh'd better have it ready for after tomorrow night when I've rubbed out Carson. Until I've done that I reckon we've no more talk about.'

'You'll get the money the following morning, when the bank opens.'

'What's a-stoppin' yuh gettin' it in now, in readiness?'

'Nothing — only I don't intend to

leave that much money lying around.'

Parry nodded, put his Stetson back on his head, and then, still holding the ledger, he went out of the office.

Immediately Binalt got to his feet and went over to the window, watched the tall, lean figure crossing the street towards Ma Falkner's and lunch — then, tapping on the glass, he brought in Brad Dugan who had been lounging on the hitch rail outside.

'Want me, boss?' he asked, chewing idly, one hand resting on the butt of his .45.

'You saw Calvert leave?' Binalt turned from the window.

'Sure. What about him?'

'We're on with a little deal together, an' for security I've had to give him an important ledger. He was carrying it with him. I want to be absolutely sure he doesn't give it to anybody else. And also I want to be sure that nobody goes to see him. That ledger mustn't change hands. I don't trust him.'

Dugan smiled cynically. 'I ain't

blamin' you, boss. Neither do I. But I thought you said he was a friend of yourn?'

'He is, but even friends can be treacherous sometimes, I reckon. You know what to do. You keep a watch on his movements and have the rest of the boys guard the trail at both ends where it leaves town. If Calvert decides to take a long ride bring him back here.'

'OK, but if it comes to that, boss, we could go get that ledger from him in no time at all.'

'No.' Binalt shook his head firmly. 'Not that. It might upset my plans. Just make sure nobody contacts him. He's stayin' at Ma Falkner's. Now get busy and don't slip up on the job.'

'OK.' Dugan turned to the door and then reflected. He gave Binalt a puzzled glance. 'Say, boss, what's happened about Carson? I thought you said you was goin' to take care of him? He's still wanderin' round as large as life. Seen him only this mornin'.'

'Suppose you leave me to handle

that,' Binalt snapped.

'Yeah, sure. Why not? I was just sort of wonderin' if Calvert was goin' to do somethin' about it. Or is his name Jeff Oakroyd?'

Binalt stared at the square-jawed face and cynical eyes for a moment. Then he gestured briefly. 'Come here Brad.'

The gunhawk released his hold on the door-knob and stepped slowly forward. Binalt was still regarding him searchingly.

'How much do you know about Calvert?' he demanded.

'I don't *know* anythin', I reckon, but I ain't plain dumb neither. I was in the high street last night when Jeff Oakroyd came ridin' through and took a shot at Carson — an' missed. I was around, too, when you said you weren't gettin' together no posse to follow him. The next thing I know a jigger about Oakroyd's size and build is teamed up with you, thicker than a mesquite bush. It sort of adds up to me — Calvert is Oakroyd, I reckon.'

'All right, he is,' Binalt said coldly. 'Who else have you told?'

'I ain't loco, boss. If there's ten thousand dollars for pickin' up that *hombre* dead or alive, I ain't exactly figgerin' to split it with nobody. I don't suppose anybody else knows — or even guesses — that he's Oakroyd.' Dugan grinned frostily. 'There's only you an' me an' him as knows it. But it's mighty nice to think there's ten thousand dollars floatin' under my nose if I choose to use my rod the right way around.'

There was naked avarice in the cold eyes: Binalt could see it plainly.

At the first chance, orders or no orders, the snaky Dugan would ram a revolver in the outlaw's back and make him ride — back to Caradoc City. He would pick up the reward and never be heard of again.

Suddenly Binalt had his own gun level, his powerful face grim.

'I ain't exactly loco either, Brad,' he said briefly. 'I can see you'd sell me out for ten thousand dollars the moment my back's turned. I'm not risking that — or you telling anybody else that Calvert is really Oakroyd. I'm making sure — right now!'

There was nothing the gunhawk could do. His hand blurred up with his own revolver, but before he could fire it two bullets hit him — one in the stomach and the other in the heart. Without voicing a sound he crashed over to the floor and lay silent. Binalt stood gazing down at him, the cordite fumes around his nostrils.

Never, he reflected, had it been more necessary to keep a man silent — and, as sheriff, with no murders to his discredit so far, he could at a pinch get away with a story of self-defence. It might never be necessary, though. It all depended on how thoroughly he rid himself of Dugan's body.

For some moments he stood waiting to see if the noise of the two shots had attracted anybody's attention, but evidently nobody had been passing at the time.

His mind was racing. Someone could easily come to his office at any minute and see him with Dugan's body. He had to get it out of town — and quickly.

At last he picked up the dead gunhawk's body and, breathing hard, carried it to the rear window of the office, from where he dropped it to the rough earth outside. At this point there was only a remote chance of anybody seeing the action. This done, Binalt went out the front way with unhurried movements, calmly untied his horse and Dugan's, and took them round to the back of his office.

He hauled the body on the saddle of Dugan's horse and then, mounted on his own animal, led Dugan's horse beside him.

In this way, taking a wide circuit of the town, he came at last to the wild, open stretches of the mesa. Here he rode for a few miles, until he had reached what he considered a safe distance from the town. Then he stopped, and pulled Dugan's body down off the horse. It dropped with a sickening thud into the dust, lying face down.

Binalt knelt and examined the murdered man. For a moment, as he turned the body over, he stared into the dead eyes, at the grotesque expression on Dugan's face. But he felt no contrition for his actions. His only regret was the thought of having pinned a possible murder rap on himself, even though he considered it most unlikely the fact would ever be discovered.

He tugged out his penknife and examined Dugan's body more closely — then received a setback. It was annoying to discover that the bullets had penetrated so deeply — being fired from such close range — that it was impossible to dig them out with only the small blade he had on him.

Then he reassured himself with the thought that nobody would ever be likely to find the corpse this far from the trail, anyway.

Binalt straightened again, slapped

Dugan's horse fiercely across the withers and watched it go scampering into the waterless, arid distances. Then he climbed back in the saddle of his bay, looked once more at the corpse of the gunhawk.

Doubts began to creep back into his mind. He cursed the fact that he'd had no opportunity to find and bring a spade with him so that he could bury the body — but there had simply been no *time* . . .

He got down again from the saddle and knelt down beside the body. He began to scrabble uselessly at the hard earth with his gun barrel and then his bare hands. He gave it up in disgust. The scorching heat of the day had baked the ground absolutely rock-solid. He scrambled to his feet and looked around him at the wilderness.

Eventually he convinced himself that no one was likely to pass this way and discover the body, at least in the short term. He could always ride out with a spade later, and, in the meantime, the scavengers might take care of the body anyway . . .

He swung himself back into the saddle of his horse and began the journey back to town.

While he rode he had plenty of time to think.

He had learned a good deal from the incident. It would not do to trust *any* of his gunhawks with the task of watching Oakroyd. Watching the trail at either end of the town would be about the limit of their assignment.

He had to watch Oakroyd himself, and be sure.

8

Parry Kelby had not, of course, the power to read Henry Binalt's mind, but he was a keen student of human nature because his job had made him that way, and it was for this reason that he felt fairly sure that somewhere, out of his line of vision, a watch would be kept on his movements to make sure the precious and incriminating ledger did not get into the wrong hands.

To test the rightness of this theory he went out after lunch, made no secret of the fact that he was putting the ledger in the saddlebag of his sorrel, and then rode out of town.

He did not go anywhere in particular: he merely went for a ride round, but little glimpses he had satisfied him that his movements were watched — and by Binalt himself. One distant view, when Binalt did not get out of sight very speedily, was enough to satisfy him. That massive figure in the black suit and hat was unmistakable.

Aware now of what he was up against, Parry realized the need of a plan for that night when he was due to visit Ann Dalman and Blake Carson at the Roaring G.

He solved it finally by a simple strategy.

Towards 9.30 he ambled out of the entrance of Ma Falkner's rooming-house and settled himself in a chair on the front porch, aware that he was fully in view for Binalt to see him — and that Binalt was watching he had not the least doubt. Though it was dark the various kerosene lamps cast quite enough illumination.

As he sprawled in the chair with his feet propped on the hitch rail, an unlighted cigarette between his lips, Parry's eyes travelled to his sorrel tied to the rail; the animal's head was nodding sleepily. Behind him in the chair Parry had the ledger, a hard, uncomfortable backrest.

For a while he sat watching the flow of people back and forth along the main street until a strolling cowhand came by.

'Got a match?' Parry asked him; and the man altered course and came up on to the porch.

'Yeah, sure . . . ' He struck it in front of Parry's unlighted cigarette. As he did so Parry blew out the match, to the man's mild astonishment, and then thrust a ten-spot bill into the man's hand.

'That's for you,' he muttered. 'An' don't tell nobody where yuh got it. I want yuh to do somethin' for me — no, don't look around yuh! Strike another match — make believe this weed won't light properly . . . '

Parry grinned tightly to himself as the man hesitated only momentarily, and then complied with his request.

'Right, now listen. Go as far as the Black Slipper and shoot your gun twice in the air. Then yell for the sheriff as hard as yuh can. Afterwards make yourself scarce. That's all, I reckon. Think yuh can do it?'

'Do it?' the cowhand scoffed. 'Sure! I reckon ten dollars is too much for a simple thing like that. 'Tain't honest.'

'Shut up an' do as I tell yuh. It's a rib I've got on. An' do it quick. Remember — tell nobody nothin'.'

'OK.' the cowhand grinned, and went down to the street again.

Parry relaxed and waited, drawing at his now smoking cigarette. It was a small thing he had planned, but he could see no reason why it should fail.

Hailed to the scene of a shooting, Binalt, whatever his wish to keep Parry under observation, would probably respond chiefly because he never lost a chance to impress the populace with his sense of duty, and also because there was the chance that the shooting might have something to do with his own personal affairs. Yes, he'd respond all right . . .

And he did. Minutes later the two

shots came, loud and clear on the night air and above the hubbub of movement on the main street. The yell the cowhand gave for the sheriff could have been heard way out on the mesa.

Parry, watching intently, saw the big, familiar, black-suited figure of Binalt dive out of a side-road opposite and mingle with an already hurrying tide of curious men and women.

With a grin Parry threw his cigarette away, jumped up with the ledger in his hand, and vaulted over the tie rail to the sorrel's saddle.

In a moment he had the ledger in the saddlebag; then, spurring the horse fiercely, he swung it down the dark space between the rooming-house and the next building.

So, with the dark and the stars for shelter he began the fast, exhilarating ride through the night wind, which in fifteen minutes brought him to the Roaring G ranch some distance beyond the town.

From what he could see of the spread

in slowly waxing moonlight it was fairly extensive, even though the corrals were empty and silent and only one light gleamed from one of the ranch house's lower windows. He removed the ledger from the saddle, tied the horse's reins to the post beside the gate and went swiftly across to the porch, knocking sharply on the screen-door.

There was an interval of a moment, and then the dim figure of Ann Dalman appeared as she opened the inner door.

'Come in,' she invited, swinging wide the screen. 'We've been expecting you.'

Parry took off his hat and followed her into the living-room. It was brighter in here than the one lighted window had led him to believe. Three oil-lamps cast a warm if subdued radiance on log walls, proofed with red clay. There was strong, serviceable furniture and skin rugs on the floor, while a small log-fire crackled in the grate.

Just risen from their chairs were two men, one obviously middle-aged with a square, good-looking face and grey hair, and the other Parry recognized as Carson, the man he had been ordered to shoot down.

'My father, and Blake Carson,' Ann introduced. 'Both of them know who you are.'

'An' I reckon we're mighty glad to meet you, Mr Kelby,' Ann's father said earnestly. 'Nice to know the law's on our side for a change.'

'If ever a man wanted kickin' out of office, it's Binalt!' Blake Carson declared fiercely, shaking hands. 'I never realized that when I got rid of Glanton I'd only done half the job.'

At close quarters he was a good-looking youngish man with a determined chin, black hair, and grey eyes.

'That's one reason why I'm election-campaigning, not so much because I want the job of mayor and sheriff but because I figure it's time the folks in Dry Acres and around it got a square deal.'

'They can have, if we follow out my

plan,' Parry said, as they all seated themselves. 'Let me explain what I've done up to now,' He nodded to the ledger he had placed carefully on the table.

'What's that?' Ann asked, puzzled. 'Is it important?'

'Definitely it is! I have there a complete record of Binalt's financial returns to date, clear-cut evidence of his dirty work which, once the authorities have looked it over, will be sufficient, I believe, for them to issue a warrant for Binalt's arrest.'

'But how in tarnation did you get hold of that?' Carson asked blankly. 'Did you steal it?'

'Hardly!' Parry gave a dry smile and then explained the details of his subterfuge. As his listeners nodded slowly he went on:

'As I had anticipated, Binalt is keeping an eye on my movements to be sure that I don't hand the ledger over to the authorities — or, for that matter to anybody else. If he saw me do that, or if

I were to be absent from town for any length of time, he'd draw his own conclusions and get out quick, probably to somewhere where we could never find him. I don't want that to happen. I want him lulled into a false sense of security until I can get help from Caradoc City.'

'But that may take some little time,' Carson mused, 'because even when the authorities get this ledger they'll have to satisfy themselves from a study of it that an arrest is compatible with law . . . '

'That's right, Mr Carson,' Parry nodded. 'If it were not for that technicality I'd have given Binalt the slip tonight and gone to Caradoc City — providing none of his gunhawks got me first — and asked for help. That would probably mean we'd lose Binalt, though . . . so I've another plan.'

'Whatever it is we're ready for it,' Carson said. 'And call me Blake.'

'Well, Blake, my job, as you'll have gathered, is to eliminate you, rub you out in your office tomorrow night, when, of course, I'll appear as Oakroyd. It's more than probable that Binalt will be watching from somewhere to satisfy himself . . . '

'So what are you going to do?' Ann asked, glancing anxiously from one man to the other.

'Relax, Miss Dalman,' Parry smiled. He looked at Blake. 'I shall shoot you with a blank cartridge and then carry you outside to my horse. I won't give Binalt the chance to find out if your heart is beating. I'll take your body on my horse out to the mesa — a plan to which Binalt has already agreed — which will give me a legitimate reason for leaving town.' He again indicated the ledger on the table.

'In the saddlebag will be that ledger. You, Blake, will take it and carry on with it on foot as far as Red Gap. There you'll hire a horse and ride to Caradoc with the ledger as fast as you can go, telling headquarters I want help the moment they are satisfied with the evidence you've brought. I shall return to Dry Acres and satisfy Binalt that you have been 'eliminated'.'

'What is there to stop either me, or Blake or even Ann — riding out to Caradoc right now with the ledger and be done with it?' the girl's father asked. 'Why all these shenanigans?'

'Because I've more than a reasonable hunch that the trails leading from both ends of Dry Acres will be watched by Binalt's hawks. That ledger is life and death to him and I'll gamble that he has men watching for any unexplained stranger or rider leaving town. I'm not taking that chance, and neither are any of you. When *I* go — with you on my horse, Blake — I'll take you to a point well beyond where any gunmen can be concealed, and I'll make sure during tomorrow to tell Binalt to have his men hold their fire if they see me. He'll be bound to agree.'

'He mightn't,' said Carson dubiously. 'Once you have 'shot' me he may think it a good idea to be rid of you, too.'

'I'll fix that. During the day I'll let

him think that the ledger is in a place where it can do one hell of a lot of damage if anything should happen to me. He'll lay off for fear of what might happen . . . Anyway, I'm prepared to take that chance. Now, is there anything you want to ask?'

'Yes,' Blake Carson said, after a moment. 'What happens if after you have 'wiped me out', Binalt offers you the money he owes and wants the ledger back? How do you figure getting around that difficulty?'

'Easily. He told me that he won't pay a cent until he's satisfied that I've disposed of you — and that wouldn't be until the bank had opened the following morning. No money, no ledger, as far as I'm concerned — and before the bank opens I'm hoping help will have come. Just as long as I can keep him in town, and fooled until we can nab him officially, I'll be satisfied. For myself, I think he'll stall in any case when it comes to paying up. If so, all the better. He won't ask for the ledger and every minute gained will count.'

Blake Carson was still not satisfied, his mind evidently still wrestling with small issues.

'There's a small but important detail, Parry. When I am in my office working I usually haven't got my jacket on — just in my shirt. Binalt knows that, and so do lots of my customers. If you shoot me and no blood or bullet hole appears it won't look too good. A bullet hole and powder mark is too tough to imitate in a few seconds . . . ' he frowned thoughtfully, then snapped his fingers.

'Got it! I'll fake a blood stain from red ink. Simple enough. I'll keep a small phial in my palm filled with red ink and break it in the right place at the right moment. I'll wear a white shirt to make it look more dramatic . . . '

'That's fine!' Parry enthused. 'The more realistic the better. Now there's one final detail to polish off the realism and make Binalt think I really am the sort of bad hat I'm supposed to be . . . '

he paused, and turned to the girl.

'You come into this, Miss Dalman. When I return to Dry Acres — and you will be able to watch for me coming without letting anybody else see you — I'll get Binalt to talk to me in the Black Slipper. You'll come in after a while and accuse me of being Jeff Oakroyd — even though I shall not then be wearing his clothes — and you'll swear that I've killed your fiancé without reason. You'll lay it on thick I am Jeff Oakroyd, just to dispel any lingering suspicions Binalt might have. Naturally you won't have any evidence and you'll probably be laughed out of the saloon — but make it look good. You, Blake, once you get to Caradoc City, will stay there until you're sent for — in time for election I hope, the result of which will be a foregone conclusion with the opposition removed.'

Carson nodded, but did not say anything. He had no intention of remaining in Caradoc City whilst others were risking their lives.

His arrangements made, Parry gave a grunt of satisfaction and rose to his feet. He picked up his hat and the ledger.

'Well, folks, that seems to be all. I shan't get in touch with you again now we know what we're doing: I mightn't even be able to sidetrack Binalt that easily a second time. Next you'll see of me, Blake, is when I 'finish you off' in your office tomorrow evening.'

'You're takin' a helluva risk, Mr Kelby — and we appreciate it,' Dalman said, shaking hands again.

'Risks are part of my life, Mr Dalman.' Parry gave a grim smile. 'Even if I don't die because of 'em I'd die without 'em — so there it is. Well, see you again . . . '

* * *

Whether Binalt was on the watch for him or not as he returned to Dry Acres, Parry did not know, nor for that matter did he particularly care. He had laid his plans and the immediate need for circumventing Binalt was over.

He left his horse at the town's livery stable, removed the ledger, and, with it under his arm, returned to Ma Falkner's rooming-house. He entered his room, struck a match and lighted the oil-lamp — then he gave a start.

Henry Binalt was seated in the shabby armchair, grim-faced, hat on the back of his head, his cheroot smouldering.

'Why don't yuh knock when yuh come in?' Parry asked him coldly, quickly assuming his Oakroyd persona, and tossing the ledger on the bed followed by his hat on top of it. 'What's the idea — or don't yuh know this is my room?'

'Sure I know, else I wouldn't be here. But you know Ma Falkner — she just doesn't care who comes or goes.'

'What in hell d'yuh *want*?' Parry snapped, his eyes narrowed.

Binalt got languidly to his feet.

'Nothin' — now. I just wanted to be

sure that you'd come back into town . . . an' with that ledger! I wouldn't like it to go some place where it shouldn't. I reckon you haven't been away long enough for it to have gone any place important, though I'm wonderin' why you took it with you.' Binalt's eyes glittered dangerously. 'There was only one sure way of finding whether you did come back and that was coming up to your room here.'

'Yuh don't think I'd have left it around for you or them owl-hooters of yours to look for, do yuh? That ledger stays beside me, Binalt, until you're good an' ready to pay up. Now get outa here: I'm turnin' in.'

Binalt gave a slow, hard smile. 'You wouldn't be after handin' me the double-cross, would you, Oakroyd?'

'The name's Calvert!'

'I reckon Oakroyd'll do for here. Ain't nobody who can hear us.'

'What do you mean — double-cross?' Parry snapped.

'I ran into somethin' odd this

evening, while I was keeping an eye on you as you sat on the porch downstairs. A cowhand fired two shots for no reason an' called for me. It was a put-up job, I'll swear, and though the guy was caught before he could escape he wouldn't say anythin'. When I got back to keepin' an eye on you you'd gone. I'm not a fool, Oakroyd: I figure that you arranged that diversion because I noticed the feller who fired the shots was the same one who gave you a match on the porch a bit earlier on. I saw you call him for just that reason. So — where'd you *go*?'

Suddenly Binalt had whipped out his gun. His dark eyes were gleaming suspiciously. Parry raised his hands slightly and shrugged.

'I ain't no objection to tellin' yuh, Binalt. I went for a ride on the mesa that's all, to get the stink o' this one-eyed town out of my nostrils.'

'I'd like to believe that,' Binalt said softly, 'but I don't! If you'd only been out on the mesa you wouldn't have needed to distract my attention like that. I figure you must have guessed I was watching you.'

'Knowing the trusting sort of guy yuh are — yes,' Parry agreed, and Binalt's face coloured darkly.

'I've been thinking,' he went on, 'that mebby I've been too soft. I think I can do without you to take care of Carson. I might even take care of it myself.'

Parry listened in uneasy wonder. What he did not know was that Binalt, already a murderer, now saw no reason why a further one should signify. If the body of Brad Dugan was ever found and the bullets were traced to him he'd swing, anyway. There was no reason now why he should not take care of Carson too, save his money, get $10,000 for turning in Jeff Oakroyd, and reclaim his ledger. His unplanned killing of Dugan had altered his mental perspective considerably.

'Yourself?' Parry repeated. 'I thought yuh was too almighty careful to do your own dirty work?'

'Never mind that; I've changed my plans. I'm also remembering that ten thousand dollars reward is offered for you, dead or alive. I've thought of a way to get it — an' be rid of you and your loco ideas about a partnership.'

This was no time for thoughts or words — but action, and Parry realized it.

He flung himself sideways as he pulled at his right-hand .38. Instantly Binalt fired, but he had been caught by surprise and had no time to aim properly. The bullet scorched past Parry's face without touching it and buried itself in the wall.

His gun out of the holster, Parry dived under Binalt's upraised gun-arm and pressed the muzzle hard in the big fellow's stomach.

'Drop it, Binalt, or I'll let yuh have it! *Drop* it!'

Slowly Binalt obeyed, put the gun back in its holster. Parry straightened up and eyed the grim face narrowly.

'Don't yuh go a-gettin' ideas like that

again, Binalt,' he said slowly. 'I'm quicker on the draw than you or your durned owl-hooters, an' yuh know it! I could pump yuh full o' lead, I reckon, but I ain't aimin' to do that because you're more useful to me alive than dead. An' I ain't forgotten that Carson killed my buddy Glanton, neither. He's my pigeon . . . so we're goin' right on with the plan, see? Just like we figured, an' if yuh ask any more questions I shan't be answerin' 'em. One last thing,' he added, and jabbed the gun hard into Binalt's stomach.

'I'll be a-watchin' yuh from now on, an' if yuh pull anythin' I'll let yuh have it first, or any of them durned gunhawks of yourn which yuh may tip off. Now get out — an' I'll be over to your office in the mornin' for a quiet, cosy little chat. There's things I'll want done afore I polish off Carson.'

Binalt hesitated, looking desperately at the ledger. Then Parry's .38 prodded him again.

'Go on — out! An' it ain't no use yuh

lookin' at that ledger. I'm a-stickin' to it, an' what's more I'll so fix it that only the authorities can find it if anythin' should happen to me. Think that one over, Binalt.'

Tight-lipped, Binalt picked up his hat, turned, and went without a word. When the door had closed Parry locked it, reholstered his gun, and whistled to himself.

It had been a tough few minutes and nearly all his plans had come within an ace of being blown sky-high. From now on he would have to be wary for the slightest sign of a treacherous move — unless his threat concerning the ledger had the desired effect of making Binalt hold his hand. He had intended making the threat, anyway: the opportunity to do it convincingly had simply arrived sooner than he had anticipated.

'But what makes him so willing to take on a murder job when before he wouldn't touch it?' Parry mused to himself and shook his head. 'Kind of queer, that. Makes it look as though

he's got nothing to lose if he does
— and far as I know he's no other
murder rap round his neck so far.'

He thought about it for a long time,
reached no conclusion, and finally set
about the task of retiring. When he got
into bed the ledger was under his pillow
beside the .38s.

9

At ten o'clock the following morning Parry strode into Binalt's office and kicked the door shut behind him. Binalt, working at his desk, chewed his cheroot from one side of his mouth to the other and looked up menacingly.

'Well, what d'you want?' he asked shortly.

'I've things to fix with yuh, Binalt, afore I takes on the job of rubbin' out Carson tonight.' Parry leaned on the desk top and cuffed up his hat.

'I've been noticin',' he went on, looking about the office and then through the window, 'that there ain't signs of your gunhawks around — either last night or this mornin'. I can see the main street from my window at Ma Falkner's, remember, an' I made it my business to look. No sign even of that owl-hooter who usually hangs around yuh — Brad Dugan.'

'Well?' Binalt's mouth tightened. A muscle twitched in his cheek. 'What of it?'

For a moment he was disturbed by the thought that 'Oakroyd' knew something, but the next words relieved him.

'I've been thinkin' — there's only one explanation for them bein' outa town. I'll gamble they're watchin' the trail both ways outa town in case I try and skip, huh?'

'Right! Exactly right.' Binalt took his cheroot from his mouth and set it in the ash-tray. 'Any objections? I'm not takin' the risk of you — or anybody else — leavin' the town with that ledger of mine. My boys have got orders to stop anybody they see. There ain't a stage due for two days so nobody can do anything *that* way. And there's only one trail from either end of town that anybody *can* take. Just a little precaution . . . Want to make somethin' of it?'

'Nope — but I'll tell yuh this much. Yuh can call off those boys of yourn tonight after I've rubbed out Carson, otherwise they're likely to get me . . . an' if they did that,' Parry added, with a cold grin, 'that ledger would sure take a fast trip to Caradoc City by a way yuh'd never think of.'

Sheer bluff of course, but the mystery was sufficient to convince Binalt. His private plans for disposing of Oakroyd were completely hamstrung by the ever-hanging threat of the ledger. It was his Achilles' heel and sword of Damocles rolled into one.

'So,' Parry finished, lighting a cigarette, 'yuh'd better play the game my way, Binalt, or it'll be just too bad.'

'I can see that,' Binalt admitted sullenly. 'OK, you're smart. I like a smart man. I reckon I lost my head last night in Ma Falkner's.'

'I reckon yuh did.' Parry nodded. 'Yuh'll call off those men of yourn at sunset. 'Bout that time I'll — '

'I'll not call 'em off, Oakroyd,

because I'm not that crazy. There ain't nothin' to stop you fixing it with somebody to get that ledger out of town the moment the guard's off. I'm not risking it. What I will do is tell my boys to hold their fire if they see a rider carrying a man across his horse. Since it'll be moonlight by that time they'll see clearly enough.'

'OK,' Parry assented. He had more or less expected this would be the final arrangement, for which very reason he had not agreed to Carson, Ann Dalman, or her father taking the ledger themselves.

'I've also been thinkin',' Binalt added slowly, 'that I might as well ride with you from town here and make sure you do a proper job of disposin' of Carson's body after you've shot him.'

Parry waited, his easy smoking not in the least betraying the sudden consternation he felt.

'Only,' Binalt said at last, reflecting, 'mebby I'd better not. If I was seen anywhere near Carson or the masked desperado the folks'd put two and two together. The best I can do is see his body after you've shot him. Just to make sure you don't double-cross.'

'Why in hell would I do that? I've a personal score to settle with Carson, don't forget. An' I've too much likin' for twenty-five hundred dollars to do that anyway,' Parry told him, straightening up. 'That bein' settled, I'll go and get myself some fresh air. I'll take care o' Carson tonight, don't yuh sweat.'

He strode out of the office and into the heat of the street again. Though he felt reasonably sure that Binalt was too leery to attempt anything in the way of gun-play upon him he did realize the necessity for not even giving him the chance.

So he returned to Ma Falkner's and stayed in his room for the rest of the day, appearing only at meal-times. The rest of the time he spent in writing out a full official report of his activities to date, to be turned in at headquarters when the whole business was finally completed. The only other job he did was prepare a blank cartridge in his right-hand .38 for Carson to receive.

In spite of the roundabout way in which he had gone to work he felt fairly sanguine of the outcome. The only thing now that could blow the whole thing higher than a kite was the unknown factor, but as far as he could foresee none was likely to arise.

The report he put inside a sealed envelope in the ledger, then, in the late evening, he dressed in Oakroyd's clothes, thereby, without the face-mask, not looking any different from any other cowpuncher. With the ledger concealed in the mackinaw he carried under his arm, he went across to the livery stable for his sorrel.

In the semi-gloom of the stable he transferred the ledger to the saddlebag, and put on the mackinaw — which Binalt had loaned him with the 'Calvert' outfit — over his shirt. It was probable that once again Binalt had been watching everything, and so the donning of a mackinaw for the cold of the night desert air would seem quite logical.

This done, Parry swung into the saddle and jogged the horse gently into the high street, drawing to a halt eventually in the narrow space between two buildings from where he could watch Carson's store and office.

The star-blazoned darkness descended swiftly over the town and by degrees the kerosene lamps began to glow. Parry remained more or less motionless on his horse, leaning on the saddle horn.

The men and women drifting along the street or the boardwalks cast him a glance as they passed, but nothing more. There was no reason to be suspicious of a cowpuncher lounging on his cayuse, watching the ebb and flow of people.

Then at last the darkness was deep enough. There would be a brief period before the eastern silver turned to full moonlight.

Behind Parry, the landscape was in

gathered mists. Before him, the main street had almost cleared of people, who had either gone home or else into the Black Slipper.

Parry nodded to himself and neck-reined his horse forward until he came to the lighted office of Blake Carson. He dismounted, fastened his horse to the tie rack, and glanced about him. Almost immediately the powerful figure of Binalt loomed out of the flaring lamplight.

'Still not trustin' me, huh?' Parry asked him bitterly.

'You an' a sidewinder both, Oakroyd. All right — get busy and kill Carson.'

Parry hesitated. He had not expected that Binalt would make himself so obvious; rather he had expected that he would creep from some hiding-place when Parry had gone into the office. There was just a chance that left alone out here he might look in the saddlebag, and then . . .

'You're takin' a risk stickin' out here, Binalt,' Parry told him. 'Better come in with me an' make sure I don't double-cross you.'

'Yeah? An' supposin' you miss Carson an' he can tell everybody else afterwards that I was beside you? How'd that look?'

'I ain't a-goin' to miss,' Parry retorted, whipping out his right-hand .38. 'An' you're so sure I might cross yuh up I'm a-givin' yuh the chance to take it back. Come on inside afore you're spotted.'

A glimpse of three cowpunchers advancing idly from up the street made up Binalt's mind for him. He nodded and Parry gave a sigh of relief under his breath. Loosening his neckerchief he drew it up until it was level with his eyes, and then marched into Carson's office.

Blake Carson glanced up casually in the lamplight and considering he knew what was coming he was very convincing. He raised his hands, keeping his fists doubled.

As arranged, his white shirt front was

nakedly clear in the lamplight.

'What's the idea?' he snapped, as Parry kicked the door shut, and his eyes darted momentarily to Binalt.

'Just that I don't like your opposition, Carson,' Binalt said, tugging out his own gun. 'I've decided to take care of you, Carson — make sure you don't win that election.'

Carson's alarm was no longer assumed: it was genuine. There would be no play-acting about it if Binalt fired — a fact of which Parry was aware, too. His left hand closed down on Binalt's gun firmly and forced him to lower it.

'Take it easy, Binalt,' he muttered. 'You gone crazy? I'm a-doin' this job. I've told yuh often enough that settlin' with the killer o' Glanton's my personal business. An' if yuh get *your* bullets in Carson and they're found an' traced, what then?'

'I'm not such a durned fool as to fire,' Binalt answered sourly. 'I'm just makin' sure this guy doesn't take advantage of any false moves you might make. Get on with it, Oakroyd! We're wasting time.'

'Yes, I know you're Oakroyd,' Carson snapped, leaping up. 'And for that I — '

Parry fired.

Instantly Carson gasped, clapped his hand to his heart and held it there, stared fixedly for a moment, and then crashed over to the floor. Binalt glanced about him as Parry dived forward and hauled the 'dead' man to his feet.

Binalt looked at the spreading red stain on the white shirt and then, his own safety paramount in his mind, gazed through the window.

'Hurry it up!' he ordered. 'Somebody might have heard that shot. What about him — is he finished?'

'Yeah — sure. As dead as Glanton!' Parry said grimly. He hauled Carson on to his shoulder and opened the office door. Apparently nobody had heard the shot as the main street was still almost deserted.

'Let's take a look at him,' Binalt said,

as Parry flung the 'body' over his saddle.

Parry did not give him the chance. He whipped up the reins from the tie rail and leapt into the saddle.

'There ain't no time for that, Binalt' he snapped. 'He's finished, I tell yuh — yuh can see that stain right over his heart for yourself. Even if there's a thread o' life left I reckon the desert'll soon discourage it. Yuh told your men to hold their fire?'

'I did, yes.'

'OK. I'll be back as soon as I've gotten rid of this body. See yuh later — in the Black Slipper.'

Parry did not wait a second longer. Spurring his horse he sent it diving forward along the main street, from which he swung at the first available turning — and so, keeping well to the back of the town and pulling down his neckerchief-mask as he went, he galloped the horse with all speed along the trail he was forced to take at first, then out into the moonlit mesa.

Gradually, when the trail was left behind, Carson began to straighten up a little, but not too much for there was no telling where exactly the gunhawks might be planted, and to see the 'corpse' sitting up would be fatal.

'Everything OK?' he asked, his voice shaken by the motion of the horse against his stomach.

'Couldn't be better,' Parry told him, grinning. 'The ledger is in the saddle-bag, complete with my instructions and report. Once we've got as far as is safe you've nothing to do but walk on with the ledger to Red Gap, get a horse, and go on to Caradoc. Ann knows exactly what to do, doesn't she?'

'She sure does. And she's looking forward to it. She says she's going to make that accusation extra good for your sake.'

'Good. Now keep quiet in case our voices carry. I'll take you half-way to Red Gap: that won't leave too big a distance for you to walk, and it'll also take you well beyond the range of any gunmen.'

For twenty minutes of hard riding Parry said nothing more, the horse racing across the vast expanse.

'Say,' Carson said at last, in a wondering voice, 'turn back a minute. I just saw somethin' that looked mighty strange. I wouldn't swear to it in this light, but it looked like a body!'

'A body!' Parry's voice was startled. 'I didn't see anything . . .'

'Mebby not, but you're lookin' ahead: in this position I have to look at the ground. I'm sure I saw something lyin' in the sage back there.'

Parry swung the horse round and in three minutes of slow trotting they had come to the spot where Carson had thought he'd seen something. He slid from the saddle and hurried forward, Parry close behind him.

There had been no mistake. The stiff, dew-soaked body of a man was lying there, his guns still in his holsters.

'Sufferin' cats, it's Brad Dugan!'

Carson gasped blankly. 'Dead as a skunk. He used to be Binalt's right-hand man.'

'Yeah.' Parry, frowning, went down on his knees and stared at the dead face in the moonlight. 'So *this* is where he got to! Ways out on the mesa where only a hundred-to-one chance would let anybody see him before the scavengers took care of him — and likely as not nobody *would* have seen him unless they were looking at the ground as you were. Blake, this tells me a lot.'

'It does? How? Who do you think did it?'

'Binalt, I'll wager. In fact, I'm sure of it.'

'But how can you be so certain?' Carson asked, wonderingly.

'Last night Binalt told me he'd thought of takin' care of you himself,' Parry said deliberately. 'I had a hard job to convince him that I should do it, according to our plan. I *wondered* why he'd so suddenly become quite uncon-cerned about committing murder: the thing's clear now. He'd already shot Dugan here and doesn't care now if he shoots anybody else.'

'Looks like you're right,' Carson muttered. 'Wonder why?'

'No idea. But it happened.'

'And it makes Binalt a murderer — if we can prove it.'

Parry made no answer. He was busy stripping off the shirt from the body. This done he looked at the bared chest intently and then he said:

'There are two bullet wounds here, Blake, but it looks as though Binalt — if it was he — didn't dig them out. Mebby they're in too deep. From the powder-marking it was close-range fire, an' that would drive the bullets in mighty deep.' Parry stood up again, thinking.

'Something just occurs to me,' he went on. 'We may have the very proof we need. Last night in my room at Ma Falkner's there was some gunplay and Binalt fired at me. His bullet went in the wall of my room and I thought no more about it. But if that bullet matches the two in this body, scoring for scoring, Binalt's got himself a rope round his neck!'

'Right!' Carson breathed. 'Right enough. And considering the number who've suffered and been killed through his orders it's no more than he deserves. What do you reckon we should do?'

Parry decided immediately. At the back of his mind there had so far been the nebulous fear that the authorities might not consider the ledger sufficient evidence for arresting Binalt — but this was different. Murder would bring the authorities over like a flock of vultures.

'We're taking the body as far as half a mile from Red Gap,' he said. 'It'll be slow for us because it's one hell of a load for the horse, but it's the only way. Once that's done you'll get a horse as arranged. The only difference will be that as well as taking the ledger into Caradoc you'll take Dugan as well. Once you're there tell the authorities to dig the bullets out of Dugan's body. They can send a ballistics expert back with the boys to Dry Acres, and by that time I'll have the other bullet from the wall of my room for comparison. If they match — that's that! Now come on: Binalt will be thinking I've skipped if I don't show up quick.'

Between them they hauled the corpse on to the sorrel and fell to the grisly task of roping it into position — the only method of holding it since advanced rigor mortis made it impossible to bend it.

Then, both of them doing their best to sit as lightly as possible on the overburdened beast, they continued across the moonlit mesa in the direction of the nearest town of Red Gap.

10

It was nearing eleven o'clock when Parry rode back swiftly into town. For just a moment as he entered the main street he caught a glimpse of a slender figure in the shadow of a doorway.

He guessed it was Ann Dalman even though he made no attempt to be certain. Time would not allow of it for one thing, and for another the last thing he dared risk was to be seen with her.

At this hour, with the Black Slipper due to shut before long, the main street was almost empty. Not that it really mattered, for Parry was pretty certain that nobody had seen his departure with Carson from the far end of the street.

He rode straight to Ma Falkner's and went to his room. Quickly he changed from his 'Oakroyd' outfit into 'Calvert', and then set about probing the wall with his jackknife. In a few minutes he had the bullet in his palm and examined it intently.

With a grim smile Parry put the bullet carefully in his shirt pocket — now secured again — beside his marshal's badge, then, grabbing his hat, he left the rooming-house and went across the street to the Black Slipper.

There were one or two glances towards him as he paused just inside the saloon and looked about him. The place was full, reeking with the odour of liquor, tobacco-fumes, and kerosene. The tables were mostly filled with men and women and the distant faro and roulette-layouts were working overtime. Parry turned and looked towards the bar. Binalt was standing there, a whiskey glass in his hand, gazing towards him. He eyed Parry darkly as he came up.

'You took long enough, didn't you?' he demanded querulously.

'Give me a whiskey,' Parry told the barkeep, and he half consumed it before he answered.

'I took my time, Binalt, because I like makin' sure. Never know what yuh might find out on the mesa, I reckon.'

If Binalt read anything into the words he did not betray it.

'What did you do?' he asked, setting down his glass and pulling out a cheroot.

'Buried Carson out on the mesa. I had a small-handled spade in my saddlebag. There ain't nobody ever a-goin' to find him: I'll see to that. An' that bein' done I reckon we've a little matter to settle. Forty thousand dollars belongs to me — as well as half of everythin' else yuh make out of this cockeyed town.'

'You'll get it — when the bank opens tomorrow. You don't think I'd carry that sort of money around with me, do you?'

'Nope. I remember yuh sayin' yuh wouldn't trust leavin' it in your safe. OK, it can wait — but not one minute beyond bank opening . . . '

Parry broke off and glanced towards

200

the batwings. They opened and shut as Ann Dalman entered the saloon.

Her face was determined, her mood entirely disciplined for the occasion. Parry waited, in readiness for the fireworks to come.

The girl glanced about the crowded room and then came across to the bar swiftly.

'Where's Blake Carson?' she demanded angrily.

Parry looked surprised and Binalt mechanically refilled his glass with whiskey.

'Blake Carson?' Parry repeated. 'Should I know?'

'You ought to! You shot him!'

Binalt gave a start and put his glass down again. Parry's eyes strayed to him and then back to the girl. The attention of all the men and women in the room was centred now on the trio beside the bar counter.

'You shot him, I tell you!' Ann went on passionately. 'I was going to meet him tonight after he had left his office. I was right on my way there when I heard a shot. I didn't come and investigate because I was scared I might get some lead into me, too. Next thing I saw was you, Mr Jeff Oakroyd . . . '

'Oakroyd!' gasped somebody.

' . . . carrying Blake Carson away on your horse,' the girl finished.

'What *else* did you see?' Binalt snapped.

'Just that!' The girl's eyes flamed as she glanced at him. 'Isn't it enough? What are you going to do — let this outlaw fool you into thinking he's somebody else?'

Binalt drew hard at his cheroot and said nothing.

The main thing that was evident to him was that the girl was lying and had not really seen anything, otherwise she would have seen *him* as well, and this was hardly a fact that, in her present mood, she'd suppress. Parry, too, had already observed the unwitting mistake she was making and, as well as he could, tried by expressions to make her soft-pedal — but she didn't.

Knowing what was expected of her she went further and deeper into the mess. 'Whether or not you're in cahoots with this bandit or not, I don't know, Sheriff,' she went on. 'As a man of law I reckon you oughtn't to be — but he's Oakroyd, I tell you. Jeff Oakroyd, a wanted criminal.'

'What kind of a game *is* this?' Parry demanded. 'My name's Calvert — Joe Calvert — an' if yuh want my opinion you're crazy! I never done anythin' to Carson an' I don't know who did. In fact, come to think on it, I don't hardly know the guy.'

'That's right,' Binalt agreed, with a grim look. Then he grasped the girl's arm tightly. 'You're lyin', Miss Dalman! You didn't see *anythin*' tonight outside Carson's, an' if you did it wasn't Calvert here. I'll gamble you never saw anything!'

'I tell you I did!' Ann retorted, giving Parry a somewhat helpless look as she sensed something had gone wrong somewhere. 'And, besides . . . ' she broke off and felt quickly in her shirt pocket.

'Anyway, this *is* Jeff Oakroyd! Look at this for yourself! Compare the features and the build. Make him put his neckerchief round his face and see what you get!'

She pulled out the information leaflet Parry had given her and he gave a violent start. He made a grab at it but Binalt got it first. Dark fury crossed his face as he looked at it. Parry's hand slid in readiness to the butt of his gun and he gave the girl a despairing glance. In her anxiety to do the thing properly she had completely overdone it.

'Where did you get this?' Binalt grated at her.

'What does that matter? There's dozens of those reward-notices scattered about the district. What's one more?'

'This one,' Binalt said, measuring his words, 'is an *official* one — the kind they issue from police headquarters. It couldn't have come from any other place. By all the devils, now I — '

'Take it easy!' Parry interrupted, relapsing into his own voice and yanking out his gun. 'Don't get excited, Binalt. Things have worked out a bit faster than I'd intended, that's all.'

Binalt clenched his fists, his dark eyes glittering.

'Now I get it! This gal here was tipped off to tell a story of what happened tonight — an' it's got so many holes in it you can see right through it. *You* told her to tell it!'

'What you really mean is that had she been watching tonight she would have seen you leaving Carson's office, too, eh?' Parry asked drily.

'Shut up, you damned fool! Do you want the whole place to hear you?'

'Why not? They will sooner or later. Might as well be sooner, I reckon ... That was a bit over-zealous of you, Miss Dalman,' Parry added, glancing at her. 'Handing round a note exclusively from headquarters just gives things away. Anyway, Binalt, for your information I'm Parry Kelby, and here's my official position.'

Parry exhibited his marshal's badge, then returned it to his pocket. From the men and women at the tables came murmurs of surprise and out of the corner of his eye Parry saw four or five of Binalt's gunhawks come drifting across with their hands on their guns. The very thing Parry had sought to avoid — the job of tackling this whole business alone — had descended upon him.

'I — I just didn't realize . . . ' Ann whispered, keeping close beside him and glancing nervously about her.

'What about Carson?' Binalt demanded. 'What's this damned girl talking about?'

'You needn't waste time trying to convince these folks that you had nothing to do with that,' Parry answered, with a glance at the faces turned in their direction. 'What you really mean is: after you'd told me to kill Carson, what did I do with him? The answer's mighty simple. I shot him with a blank and he smeared red ink on himself. At this moment he's in Caradoc City, alive, and with that precious ledger of yours. He's also got something *else* with him that's mighty valuable . . . '

Binalt spat out his cheroot. 'Meanin' what?'

'The body of Brad Dugan!'

11

There was a long, deadly silence. Then Binalt gave a short laugh.

'Brad Dugan, eh? You're not suggestin' I killed him, are you? Why, anyone could have done it. He had plenty of enemies, I reckon.'

'The main concern of the authorities will be that he has two bullets in his body, Binalt, and if they should match with the bullet you fired at me in Ma Falkner's last night, *and* with those guns you're wearing, you know where you'll finish up. I don't definitely know yet if you did kill him or for why, but I reckon mistrust would be as good a motive as any.' He broke off as he watched the expression on Binalt's face. His look of rage was definitely touched with fear — and guilt.

'In any case,' Parry continued, the assembly in the saloon now hanging on his every word, 'you're in for trouble with the extortion you've been practising and these folks who've been soaked by you might as well know it. The joy-ride's over, Binalt. I'd intended waiting for official word from Caradoc, but now my hand's been forced. You're under arrest. Come on — to your horse outside.'

Parry had hardly finished speaking before a gun exploded with deafening force near at hand. At the same instant his revolver was blown clean out of his fingers and went spinning across the floor. He swung round, nursing his stinging but untouched hand. To the rear, round the curve of the bar-counter, three of the gunhawks who had been sidling up from the crowd were now standing, guns pointed.

'Take it easy, Kelby, or whatever your durned name is,' one of them warned. 'The boss ain't goin' nowhere until he's good an' ready — an' them orders applies to the rest of you!' the gunhawk added, contemplating the men and women at the tables. Most of them, though astounded at the revelations, were quite ready to believe them. A mayor who could soak them as Binalt had done, and a sheriff who could shut his eyes so completely to law and order, was in their estimation capable of anything. Most of them would gladly have given Parry the help he needed, but six loaded guns in the hands of three desperate men were powerful deterrents.

'It looks,' Binalt said, tugging out his own guns and covering Parry with them, 'as though you're not quite so smart as you thought, Kelby. Mind you, I'll admit you had me fooled: I really did think you were Oakroyd. What happened to him, anyway?'

Parry, realizing now that his only chance lay in stalling as long as possible, took his time over answering. Then he said:

'He killed himself accidentally. Fell over a cliff into a river and I took his place . . . ' Parry turned deliberately and looked at the silent, set-faced men and women around the tables.

'For your benefit, folks, you might as well know that this precious mayor of yours has been gypping you so completely because there's gold on this land. I've seen traces of it, but where the *real* gold is only Binalt knows. Now you know why he forced you into selling — so he could buy up cheap.'

'That's right,' Binalt agreed easily. 'An' I ain't telling where that gold is, neither. What's more, Kelby, I'm going to take care of you in the good old-fashioned way, and when the authorities come here I'll have your body so far from this town it'll never be found. As for that bullet you got from your hotel room for checking . . . Well, I'll simply ditch these guns of mine and use fresh ones. They won't pin nothing on me.'

'You're a bigger fool than I took you for, Binalt,' Parry replied. 'All these people are now witnesses to what is practically your confession. You can't silence all of them!'

'With my grip on this town unshaken you'd be surprised what I can do,' Binalt retorted. 'A flock of sheep like these folk and a dozen strong men on the right end of shootin'-irons are mighty powerful persuaders. As for that ledger I'll tell 'em that you faked it.'

'You can't do that, Binalt. You're pipe-dreaming. You're nailed, and you know it!'

If Binalt did know it — which in his heart he did — he did not admit it because his egotism and a cold, devouring fury would not let him. He turned and looked at the men and women.

A change had come over them. Here and there men were moving from table to table, apparently following some whispered plan of their own.

The chief reason for the change in attitude had obviously been caused by the reference to gold. The knowledge that many of them might be perched over a fortune made the danger of levelled guns seem unexpectedly trivial. What was even more important — only *Binalt* possessed the knowledge of where the actual gold lay!

And suddenly the tense, heavy calm broke — in an unexpected way. Evidently acting upon a prearranged signal three of the men seated at a nearby table jumped up simultaneously and raised the table with them. With their united strength they flung it at the three gunmen at the bar-counter. It acted both as a shield against their bullets as they fired wildly, and the heavy mass knocked them flying as it crashed into them.

The advantage gained, pandemonium broke loose. Binalt fired his own guns, but simultaneously Parry lashed up his foot and kicked the aim towards the ceiling. Then he wrenched the guns from Binalt's hands and closed with him, forcing his broad, powerful back against the counter edge.

Ann Dalman was not without courage of her own. She took the only course which seemed open to her and snatched up a whiskey bottle from the counter, bringing it down hard on the head of the nearest gunman as, recovering from the table onslaught, he swung round to point his gun. Instantly he collapsed again, whiskey and blood intermingling down his face from an ugly headwound as he fell his length.

Ann stooped and whipped the guns from him, held them in readiness to protect herself.

Gunplay was useless now, however. It was impossible to tell the difference between friend and foe. The thing had developed into a free-for-all, some merely taking care of old scores and others determined to help Parry by incapacitating all the friends of Binalt. Those who wanted to get at Binalt himself and hammer the truth out of him concerning the gold's location gave up the idea when they saw that Parry was already taking care of it.

With both hands on the big fellow's throat Parry forced him hard against the counter-edge. Behind the bar the barkeep had vanished, presumably to join whichever side he now supported. A chair sailed through the air and smashed into the mirrors and bottles of the back-bar.

'Out with it, Binalt!' Parry snapped. 'Where's that bonanza? And by the way, this part's unofficial. As an official of the law I can't beat you up — but as a plain, ornery man determined to see justice done I'm ready to whip the hide off you. So start talking, damn you!'

He landed a hammer blow into Binalt's face and Binalt felt his head sing. He shook it stubbornly — then, goaded by the torture the length of his spine, he forced himself forward suddenly by sheer main strength, bracing his feet against the base of the counter. Taken off-balance Parry stumbled backwards, into a table and half across it.

Instantly Binalt was on top of him and they closed round each other.

Jerking one hand free Binalt slammed

a crushing fist into Parry's face that dazed him for a moment. Another followed it and he tasted the salt of blood. Then he doubled up his knee and the impact took Binalt in the stomach.

He was heaved upwards and backwards, got his legs entangled in those of a chair and half fell over. Parry finished it for him by landing a sledge-hammer blow on the back of his thick neck. With a gasp Binalt fell flat, half stunned by the blow.

He had no chance to rest for Parry seized his collar and whirled him to his feet, shot out his fist with piston-rod force and sent him staggering amidst the tables at the further end of the long room. Somehow he kept his balance and with murderous fury on his face came charging forward again, stopping momentarily to pick up a bottle from a table and smash it in two.

With his deadly weapon in a tight grip he dived, and Parry shot out his hand to protect himself. A revolver exploded somewhere and the half-bottle was blown to bits in Binalt's hand, the bullet sending living fire through his arm as it went clean through his palm. White-faced, watching attentively for another chance, was Ann Dalman.

The instant Binalt saw that she was the cause of his anguish he switched his attentions, lashed out his left fist and struck her hard across the face.

With a gasping cry she sprawled on the floor, the gun flying from her hand. She lay still where she had fallen, knocked clean out by the force of the vicious blow.

'You dirty, stinking skunk — beating on a girl,' Parry breathed. 'You need teaching some chivalry and by hell you're going to have it!'

He lashed out his fist, aiming at Binalt's stomach — and missed. His threats had alerted the big man. Instead he met a mule-kick on the side of his jaw that rocked him on his heels. Another one followed it and he stumbled blindly.

In spite of his pain and haziness part of his mind noticed that the rest of the fight had quietened. The gunhawks had been overcome and the remainder of the saloon's habitués had formed into a wide circle, giving plenty of room and yelling encouragement. Ann's still unconscious figure had already been carefully lifted and borne out of the danger area.

'Make him tell us where that gold is, marshal!' somebody yelled.

'Carve your initials on his ugly fanny! That's about the best thing for a dirty chiseller like him . . . '

The shouts goaded the desperate Binalt to a final effort. Suddenly he sprang, and Parry collapsed under the weight, trying to protect his head from the rain of blows that descended upon it from Binalt's remaining sound fist. As he lay thus, taking savage punishment, he saw near him an overturned chair.

He shot out a hand towards it, gripped it, and heaved it upwards and backwards, smashing it down with crashing force across Binalt's head and shoulders. It had the desired effect of halting the onslaught for a moment or two and in that time Parry had heaved upwards and got on his feet.

With one terrific right-hander he sent Binalt crashing into the rickety piano. Piano and man collapsed in a cracking mass of wood and discord.

'Now!' Parry breathed, leaping forward and pinning Binalt's struggling figure to the floor by planting both knees in his chest. 'This is where you start talking, Binalt. You like whiskey, don't you?'

'Whiskey?' Binalt repeated through battered lips, glaring. 'What the hell are you talkin' about?'

'Whiskey somebody!' Parry ordered. 'A dozen bottles to start with!'

Binalt struggled again but there was nothing he could do, pinned by the knees in his chest and the ensnaring wires of the wrecked piano. He watched in grim wonder as Parry took the whiskey bottle that was handed to him by barkeep Andy Parker.

'Here y'are, marshal — on the house!' Evidently, Parker had had the good sense to switch his loyalty away from his discredited employer.

Taking the half-drawn cork out with his teeth Parry raised one of the felt pegs spewed from the piano and jammed it between Binalt's upper and lower jaws. Then he began to pour the whiskey into his mouth as though down a drain.

'All the whiskey you can want, Binalt,' Parry explained. 'And an endless supply of bottles to keep you going. If you want to speak and tell us where the gold is just bang on the floor with your good hand.'

For a while Binalt suffered the punishment, gurgling frantically as he tried to consume the spirit, but by the middle of the second bottle he could stand it no longer and thumped hard on the floor. Half-choked, black-faced with fury and shortness of breath, he lay gasping hard for a moment.

'OK — OK,' he panted. 'You win. That gold strike's a yard below surface and covers half the land in Dry Acres, as far south as the Roaring G . . . '

'Our ranch!' Ann gasped, who, now recovered, was looking on with the others. 'Are you telling the truth?'

'Why else do you think I crippled you and old man Dalman with taxes?' Binalt said.

'If you're lying,' Parry muttered, raising the whiskey bottle again, 'I'll — '

'No, no, it's truth! I swear it is!' Binalt gasped, sweat streaming down his face and neck.

Parry put the bottle down and yanked out his gun. Motioning with it, he got to his feet.

'All right, Binalt — get up from the floor.'

Sullen and scowling, Binalt obeyed and found himself motioned over to the bar. He wrapped a handkerchief round his wounded hand as he moved. He cast a grim glance at his henchmen, all of them sour-faced and under the menace of levelled guns.

'You're staying right here, Binalt, until they send from headquarters,' Parry explained, perching on a table and jabbing at his cut face with his disengaged hand. 'That should be in about an hour at the very outside.'

As it happened it was sooner. Forty-five minutes later Blake Carson and the men from headquarters rode into town and, hardly protesting, so completely beaten and exhausted was he, Binalt permitted himself to be led away with his various trigger-men. Carson, after a glance round the half-wrecked saloon, raised his brows.

'So you decided to do it on your own after all?' he asked, putting an arm about Ann's shoulder as, smiling, she came hurrying to his side.

'I'd no choice,' Parry grinned. 'And I wasn't exactly alone in the fight. I guess your wife-to-be's going to figure again in another official report! That's some gal you're getting there, Blake!'

Carson flashed a startled glance at Ann.

'Tell you later.' She smiled.

'What about those bullets?' Parry asked Carson. 'Did they get them out of Dugan's body?'

'Yes, and — '

'That's all I wanted to know. Binalt has the self-same guns on him at this moment. That will settle it for him. I have the bullet from the bedroom in my shirt pocket here. What about the ledger?'

He turned to look at the new arrivals from Caradoc City, and Walt Standish stepped forward.

'Obvious extortion, Parry,' Standish said. 'In fact, I think we have Binalt nicely sewn up and finished with.'

Parry nodded. 'Good! And that's how it wants to be . . . Well, I reckon I'd better be going along with the rest of the party. Nothing more needs to be done here.'

He turned to look at Carson and Ann, who exchanged a quick glance.

'If, after you're elected sheriff, Blake,

223

you should run into more trouble, just send out a call for me. I'll always be ready to ... ' Parry broke off, astonished, as Ann Dalman suddenly disengaged herself from Carson's arm and crossed the floor swiftly.

Before Parry could guess her intention, she flung her arms around his neck and delivered a resounding kiss. A roar of delighted approval went up from the surrounding men and women of the town.

'I just wanted to say a personal thank you,' Ann whispered, as she gently disengaged herself and smiled up at the red-faced Parry. He flashed an embarrassed glance at Blake Carson, who was smiling broadly.

'Don't worry, I don't mind my fiancée kissin' you, Marshal,' Carson grinned. Stepping forward he gripped Parry's hand and shook it vigorously.

'Hell, if you wasn't a man, after what you've done for this town I'd kiss you myself!'

We do hope that you have enjoyed reading this large print book.

Did you know that all of our titles are available for purchase?

We publish a wide range of high quality large print books including:
Romances, Mysteries, Classics
General Fiction
Non Fiction and Westerns

Special interest titles available in large print are:
The Little Oxford Dictionary
Music Book, Song Book
Hymn Book, Service Book

Also available from us courtesy of Oxford University Press:
Young Readers' Dictionary
(large print edition)
Young Readers' Thesaurus
(large print edition)

For further information or a free brochure, please contact us at:
Ulverscroft Large Print Books Ltd.,
The Green, Bradgate Road, Anstey,
Leicester, LE7 7FU, England.
Tel: (00 44) **0116 236 4325**
Fax: (00 44) **0116 234 0205**

THE CHISELLER

Tex Larrigan

Soon the paddle steamer would be on its long journey down the Missouri River to St Louis. Now, all Saul Rhymer had to do was to play the last master stroke of the evening. He looked at the mounting pile of gold and dollar bills and again at the cards in his hand. Then, looking around the table, he produced the deed to the goldmine in Montana. 'Let's play poker!' But little did he know how that journey back to St Louis would change his life so drastically.